"*There's only one Leigh Brackett and there's only one Eric John Stark—both stand alone in their field!*"

—Ray Bradbury

HEROIC ADVENTURE AT ITS BEST

A dangerous light had begun to kindle in Gerd's eyes. Abruptly the hound stood still, quivering in every muscle.

Stark braced himself.

The pack, by custom, would not interfere. This was between himself and Gerd.

"Kill, Gerd," said Gelmar quietly, his hand on the hound's shoulder. "This man will lead you all to death."

And Stark said, "You cannot kill me, Gerd. Remember Flay."

The bolt of fear struck him. It shriveled his brain and turned his bones to water. But Stark held his grip. And a fierce cry came from out of his deep past: *I am N'Chaka. I do not die!*

Stark #2

THE HOUNDS OF SKAITH

Leigh Brackett

BALLANTINE BOOKS • NEW YORK

SBN 345-24230-0-125

First Printing: October, 1974

Printed in the United States of America

BALLANTINE BOOKS
A Division of Random House, Inc.
201 East 50th Street, New York, N.Y. 10022
Simultaneously published by
Ballantine Books, Ltd., Toronto Canada

For Michael and Hilary Moorcock

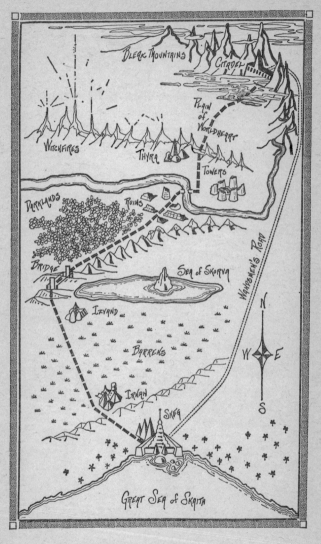

Stark's journey to the Citadel (*The Ginger Star*)

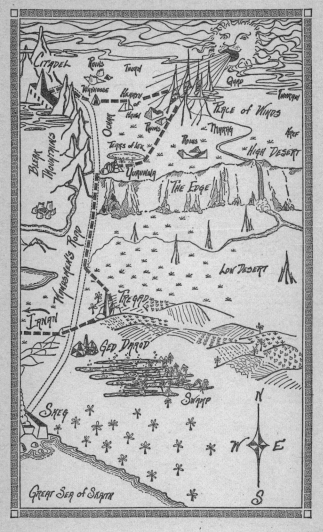

Stark's return to Irnan (*The Hounds of Skaith*)

1

In her great hall, deep in the mountain heart of the glimmering Witchfires, Kell à Marg Skaith-Daughter sat upon the dais. Her throne was carved from rich brown rock the color of loam—the shape of it was a robed woman, seated to hold Skaith-Daughter on her knees, her arms curved protectively, her head bent forward in an attitude of affection. Kell à Marg sat with her hands on the hands of Skaith-Mother, and her slim white-furred body gleamed against the dark stone.

Below, at the foot of the dais, Yetko the Harsenyi sweated in his heavy garments, keeping his eyes averted from the Presence. He was overwhelmed by the crushing weight of mountain above him and by the labyrinthine strangeness of the House of the Mother, of which this luminous white chamber was the core and center. He was overwhelmed by being there at all. Yetko and his people had traded with these Children of Skaith-Our-Mother for generations, but the trading was done in a place outside the sacred House and never by such exalted ones as were gathered here—the Clan Mothers and the counselors, the Diviners, Skaith-Daughter herself—all glittering in their fine harness and jeweled badges of rank. No other Harsenyi had ever stood where he was standing. Yetko knew that his being here was neither right nor normal, and he was afraid. But this was a time for fear and for fearful happenings, a time of breaking and sundering. He had already beheld the unthinkable. His having been brought here was surely a part of the madness that walked upon the world.

Kell à Marg spoke. Her voice was musical, with a sound of bells, but it was a voice of power nonetheless.

"You are the headman of the village?"

They both knew that she meant the permanent camp on the other side of the Plain of Worldheart. There was no other. The Harsenyi were nomads, carrying their houses with them as they moved. Yetko said:

"I am."

He was uneasy with these creatures, terrified lest he show it. Their forebears had been human, even as he was, but by some lost magic of the ancients their bodies had been altered so that they might live and be happy in these beautiful sunless catacombs, the protecting womb of the goddess they worshipped. Yetko was a child of Old Sun and the wide cruel sky; he could not understand their worship. The fine white fur that covered them disturbed him. So did their smell, a faint dry pungency. Their faces were distorted subtly from what Yetko considered the human norm—noses too blunt, jaws too prominent, eyes too large and glowing in the lamplight.

"From our high northern balconies," said Kell à Marg, "we have seen flames and smoke on the other side of the plain, behind the mists. Tell us what has happened."

"One came," said Yetko. "He overthrew the Lords Protector. They fled from him through the passes of the Bleak Mountains, along the road to Yurunna; and he burned their Citadel that has been since before the Wandering, so that only the empty walls still stand."

A sigh went around the hall, a sound of astonishment and shock.

Kell à Marg said, "Did you see this person?"

"I saw him. He was very dark and tall, and his eyes were like the ice that forms over clear water."

Again the sigh, this time with a note of vicious hatred.

"It was Stark!"

Yetko glanced sidelong at Skaith-Daughter. "You know him?"

"He was here, a prisoner of the Wandsman Gelmar. He has brought death to the House of the Mother,

2

killing two of our young men when he broke free by the northern gate."

"He will bring more death," said one of the Diviners. "The Eye of the Mother has seen this." He stepped forward and shouted at Yetko. "Why is it that the Northhounds did not kill him? Why, why? Always they guarded the Citadel from intruders. Why did they let him live?"

The Clan Mothers and the counselors echoed him, and Kell à Marg said:

"Tell us why."

"I do not know," said Yetko. "The Lords Protector told us that somehow he had slain the great king-dog Flay and taken control of the pack. They said he was more beast than man. Certainly the hounds went with him to the Citadel, and certainly they killed a number of the servants there." A deep shudder shook him as he remembered. "Certainly when he came to our camp to take riding animals from us, the Northhounds followed at his heels like puppies."

"He is not Skaith-born," said Kell à Marg. "He comes from another world. His ways are not ours."

Yetko shuddered again, partly because of her words, but mostly because of the tone in which she spoke them.

"He followed the Lords Protector?"

"Yes, with the hounds. He and another man. The other man came long before, up the Wandsmen's Road from the south. He was a captive in the Citadel." Yetko shook his head. "That one also was said to have come from beyond the sky. Mother Skaith is beset by demons."

"She is strong," said Kell à Marg, and laid her head against the breast of the brown stone woman. "There are many dangers, I believe, beyond the Bleak Mountains."

"Yes. The Hooded Men permit us to come only as far as the first wayhouse, but that is a week's journey and dangerous enough because of the Runners, which are terrible things, and because of the sandstorms. The

Hooded Men themselves are man-eaters; and the Ochar, who keep the road, are a powerful tribe."

"So that with good fortune the man Stark may die in the desert."

Yetko said, "It is likely."

"What of the Wandsman Gelmar? He left the House of the Mother with two prisoners."

"He crossed the Bleak Mountains before the attack on the Citadel. He had a Southron woman with him, and a wounded man in a litter. There were also three lesser Wandsmen and the servants."

"Perhaps I was wrong," said Kell à Marg, speaking to herself aloud, "not to let Gelmar keep the man Stark, as he wanted. But Stark was in chains. Who would have believed that he could escape our daggers, and then survive even the Northhounds?"

For the first time Yetko understood that the Presence was afraid, and that frightened him more than her strangeness or her power. He said humbly, "Please, if there is nothing more you require from me . . ."

Her dark unhuman eyes brooded upon him. "Now that the Citadel has fallen, your people are preparing to abandon the village?"

"We kept the village only to serve the Wandsmen and the Lords Protector. If they come again, so will we. In the meantime, we will only come for the trading."

"When do you go?"

"With Old Sun's next rising."

Kell à Marg nodded slightly and lifted a slender hand in a gesture of dismissal. "Take him to the outer cavern, but see that he stays there until I send word."

The two white-furred man-things who had brought Yetko from the camp to the great hall took him out again, through long hollow-sounding corridors with carved walls and ornamented ceilings and myriad doorways into dimly lighted rooms filled with half-glimpsed unknowable things. There was a smell of dust and of the sweet oil that fed the lamps. Yetko's thick feet went faster and faster, in a hurry to be gone.

Kell à Marg sat upon the knees of Skaith-Mother. She

did not move or speak; her courtiers stood waiting, silent and afraid.

At last she said, "Fenn. Ferdic."

Two lordly men stepped forward. They wore shining diadems. Their eyes, too, shone with anguish, because they knew what she was about to say to them.

Skaith-Daughter leaned forward. "The threat is greater than the man Stark. We must know the true nature and extent of the danger. Go with the Harsenyi as far south as you may, and as quickly. Go on to Skeg. Learn about these starships. Do all in your power to have them sent away to whatever suns they came from."

She paused. They bent their furred and handsome heads.

"Seek out Gelmar," she said. "He will know if Stark has somehow managed to survive the desert. And if he has, do anything, pay any price, to have him killed."

Fenn and Ferdic bowed. "We hear, Skaith-Daughter. Even this we will do, in the service of the Mother."

Men condemned to death, they withdrew to make their preparations for the journey.

First of these was a ceremony in the Hall of Joyful Rest, where the Children were laid to sleep in the embrace of the Mother. It had been so long since anyone had been forced to leave the sacred House that the officiating Diviner had difficulty in finding the proper scrolls for the ritual. The stone knife and small jeweled caskets had been untouched for centuries. Still, the thing was done at last. The severed fingers were buried in hallowed ground, so that no matter where death might overtake them on the outside, Fenn and Ferdic could know that they were not lost entirely from the tender love of Skaith-Mother.

2

Gerd thrust his massive head against Stark's knee and said, *Hungry.*

The Northhounds had been ranging ahead of the men. Born telepaths, they were able to communicate well enough for most needs; but sometimes their talk, like their minds, was overly simple.

Stark asked, *Gerd is hungry?*

Gerd growled and the coarse white fur bristled along his spine. He looked uneasily at the emptiness surrounding them.

Out there. Hungry.

What?

Not know, N'Chaka. Things.

Out there. Things. Hungry. Well, and why not? Hunger was the great constant over most of this world of Skaith, senile child of the ginger star that spilled its rusty glare out of a dim cold sky onto the dim cold desert.

"Probably a pack of Runners," Ashton said. Having been up this road as a prisoner some months before, he knew the hazards. "I wish we were better armed."

They had helped themselves to what they needed from the Citadel before Stark put it to the torch. Their weapons were of excellent quality, but Skaith's poverty-stricken technology, sliding backward through long centuries of upheaval and dwindling resources, could now offer nothing more sophisticated than the sword, the knife and the bow. Stark, being a mercenary by trade, was proficient with all these; the wars he fought in were small and highly personal affairs, involving tribes or small nations on as-yet-uncivilized worlds beyond the fringes of the Galactic Union. Simon Ash-

6

ton, who had done all his fighting years ago and in uniform, would have felt happier with something more modern.

"We have the hounds," Stark said, and pointed to a rise ahead. "Perhaps we can see something from there."

They had been driving hard ever since they left the smoking ruins of the Citadel. The passes through the Bleak Mountains led them first north and then east, and the mountain chain itself made a great bend to the southeast, so that the lower range now stood like a wall at their right hands. The Wandsmen's Road came up from Skeg straight across these eastern deserts, a much shorter route than the one Stark had followed on his own journey north from Skeg to find the hidden Citadel where Ashton was being held. He had had perforce to go first to Irnan, which was somewhat westerly, and then more westerly still, with his five comrades, to Izvand in the Barrens. After that he had made a long traverse in the creaking wagons of the trader Amnir of Komrey, who had taken them to sell for a high price to the Lords Protector, through the darklands on an ancient road. Stark's way up from Skeg had described roughly the curve of a broken bow. Now he was going south again along the straight line of the bowstring.

He whacked his shaggy little mount to a faster pace. At first, where the frozen ground was hard and stony, they had made good time. Now they were among the dunes, and the Harsenyi beasts with their sharp little hoofs were laboring.

They topped the rise and halted. By the time the westerlies came across the barrier mountains, they had dropped most of their moisture. In place of the snows on the other side there was dun-colored sand with only a splotching and powdering of white. The air was no less cold. And in all that bitter landscape, nothing moved. The cairns that marked the Wandsmen Road marched away out of sight. The Lords Protector were still well ahead.

"For old men," said Stark, "they're traveling well."

"They're tough old men. Let the beasts rest a bit, Eric. It won't help anyone if we kill them."

The exodus of the Lords Protector and their servants had taken more animals than the Harsenyi could well spare. Only fear of the Northhounds had induced them to part with three more, two for riding and one to carry supplies. They were strong little things, with thick hair that hung down as though they were wearing blankets. Bright button eyes peered through tangled fringes. Sharp horns were tipped with painted balls to prevent hooking. Their air of patient martyrdom was well spiced with malice. Still, they bore their burdens willingly enough; and Stark reckoned they would do, for the time being.

"We'll borrow some from Ferdias. But we must catch up with Gelmar before he reaches the first wayhouse. If we don't, we'll never see him, not in this desert."

"Gelmar won't be sparing his animals, either. Ferdias will have sent one of the Yur ahead to tell him what happened. He'll know you're coming after him."

Stark said impatiently, "He's traveling with a badly wounded man." Halk, the tall swordsman, albeit no friend of Stark's, had come north with him for the sake of Irnan, and he was one of the two survivors of the original five. The other was the wise woman Gerrith. They had been caught with their comrades in Gelmar's trap at Thyra, and Halk was sorely hurt in that battle.

"He must be carried in a litter. Gelmar can't travel too fast."

"I don't think you can count on that. I believe Gelmar would sacrifice Halk to keep you from taking Gerrith back. She's a vital part of their whole strategy against Irnan." Ashton paused, frowning. "Even so, I think the Wandsmen would be willing to sacrifice Gerrith if they could take you. Ferdias had the right of it, you know. It was madness to try and turn an entire planet upside down for the sake of one man."

"I've lost two fathers," Stark said, and smiled. "You're the only one I've got left." He kicked his mount forward. "We'll rest farther on."

8

Ashton followed, looking in some wonderment at this great dark changeling he had brought into the world of men. He was able to remember with vivid clarity the first time he had seen Eric John Stark, whose name then was N'Chaka, Man-Without-a-Tribe. That had been on Mercury, in the blazing, thundering valleys of the Twilight Belt where towering peaks rose up beyond the shallow atmosphere and the mountain-locked valleys held death in an amazing variety of forms. Ashton was young then, an agent of Earth Police Control, which had authority over the mining settlements. EPC was also responsible for the preservation of the aboriginal tribes, a scanty population of creatures kept so much occupied with the business of survival that they had not had time to make that last sure step across the borderline between animal and human.

Word had come that wildcat miners were committing depredations. Ashton arrived too late to save the band of hairy aboes, but the miners had taken a captive.

A naked boy, fierce and proud in the cage where he was penned. His skin was burned dark by the terrible sun, scarred by the accidents of daily living in that cruel place. His shaggy hair was black, his eyes very light in color—the clear, innocent, suffering eyes of an animal. The miners had tormented him with sticks until he bled. His belly was pinched with hunger, his tongue swollen with thirst. Yet he watched his captors with those cold clear eyes, unafraid, waiting for a chance to kill.

Ashton took him out of the cage. Thinking back on the time and effort required to civilize that young tiger, to force him to accept the hateful fact of his humanity, Ashton sometimes wondered that he had possessed enough patience to accomplish the task.

Records of Mercury Metals and Mining had given the boy's identity and his name, Eric John Stark. Supposedly, he had died along with his parents in the fall of a mountain wall that wiped out the mining colony where he was born. In fact, the aboes had found him and reared him as their own, and Ashton knew that no matter how human his fosterling Eric might look on the outside, the primitive N'Chaka was still there, close under the skin.

That was how Stark had been able to face the North-hounds and kill their king-dog Flay. That was why they followed him now, accepting him as their leader, beast to beast. Seeing the nine great white brutes running beside Stark, Ashton shivered slightly, sensing the eternal stranger in this, the only son he had ever had.

Yet there was love between them. Stark had come of his own free will, to fight his way across half this lunatic world of Skaith and free Ashton from the Lords Protector at the Citadel.

Now a long road lay before them, full of powerful enemies and unknown dangers. In his heart Ashton felt sure they would never make it back to Skeg, where the starport offered the sole means of escape. And he felt a moment of anger that Stark had put himself in this position. For my sake, Ashton thought. And how do you think I will feel when I see you die, for my sake?

But he kept this thought to himself.

When their mounts had begun to flag noticeably, Stark allowed a halt. Ashton watered the riding animals and fed them with cakes of compressed lichens. Stark fed the hounds sparingly with strips of dried meat brought from the Citadel. Gerd was still muttering about *Things,* though the landscape remained empty. The men chewed their own tough rations, moving about as they did so to stretch muscles cramped by long hours in the saddle.

Stark said, "How far have we come?"

Ashton looked at the faceless monotony of the dunes. "I'd guess we're more than halfway to the first shelter."

"You're sure there isn't any other way to go, to get ahead of Gelmar?"

"The road was laid out in the beginning along the shortest route between Yurunna and the Citadel. It hardly bends an inch in a hundred miles until it hits

10

those mountain passes. No shortcuts. Besides, if you lose the guideposts you're done for. Only the Hooded Men and the Runners know their way around the desert." Ashton drank water from a leather bottle and handed it to Stark. "I know how you feel about the woman, and I know how important it is to keep Gelmar from taking her back to Irnan. But we've all got a long way to go yet."

Stark's eyes were cold and distant. "If Gelmar reaches the wayhouse before us, he will get fresh mounts. The tall desert beasts, which are much faster than these. Am I right?"

"Yes."

"He will also see to it that there are no fresh mounts for us, and the tribesmen will be warned to look for us."

Ashton nodded.

"Perhaps, with the hounds, we might overcome those difficulties. Perhaps. But the next wayhouse is seven days beyond?"

"Not hurrying."

"And Yurunna is seven days beyond that."

"Again, not hurrying."

"Yurunna is a strong city, you said."

"Not large, but it stands on a rocky island in the middle of a fat oasis—or what passes for a fat oasis hereabouts—and there's only one way up. The wild tribesmen look upon it with lust, but it's so well guarded they don't even raid much around the oasis. The Yur are bred there, the Well-Created. Some more of the Wandsmen's nastiness; I don't believe in breeding humans like prize pigs even to be the perfect servants of the Lords Protector. The Northhounds are bred there, too, and sent north along the road to the Citadel as they're needed. How would meeting their old kennelmates and the Houndmaster affect your friends?"

"I don't know. In any case, the hounds alone would not be useful against a city."

He put away the bottle and called the pack. The men climbed again onto the saddle-pads.

"There's another good reason for hurrying," Stark said. He looked at the wasteland, at the dim sky where Old Sun slid heavily toward night. "Unless we want to spend the rest of our lives on Skaith, we had better get back to Skeg before the Wandsmen decide to send the ships away and close the starport down for good."

3

Starships were a new thing on Skaith. Only in the last dozen years had they arrived, a shattering astonishment out of the sky.

Before that, for its billions of years of existence, the system of the ginger star had lived solitary in the far reaches of the galaxy, untouched by the interstellar civilization that spread across half the Milky Way from its center at Pax, chief world of Vega. The Galactic Union had even embraced the distant little world of Sol. But the Orion Spur, of which Skaith and her primary were citizens, had remained largely unexplored.

In her young days, Skaith was rich, industrialized, urbanized and fruitful. But she never achieved spaceflight; and when the ginger star grew weak with age and the long dying began, there was no escape for her people. They suffered and died, or if they were strong enough, they suffered and survived.

Gradually, out of the terrible upheavals of the Wandering, a new social system arose.

The consul of the Galactic Union, who spent a few brief hopeful years at Skeg, wrote in his report:

The Lords Protector, reputed to be "undying and unchanging," were apparently established long ago by the then ruling powers as a sort of superbenevolence. The Great Migrations were beginning, the civilizations of the north were breaking up as the people moved away from the increasing cold, and there was certain to be a time of chaos with various groups competing for new lands. Then and later, when some stability was reestablished, the Lords Protector were to prevent a too great trampling of the weak by the strong. Their law was simple: Succor the weak, feed the hungry, shelter the homeless—striving always toward the greatest good of the greatest number.

It appears that through the centuries this law has been carried far beyond its original intent. The Farers and the many smaller nonproductive fragments of this thoroughly fragmented culture are now the greater number, with the result that the Wandsmen, in the name of the Lords Protector, hold a third or more of the population in virtual slavery, to supply the rest.

A slavery from which there was no escape, until the starships came.

Skaith was starved for metals, and the ships could bring those, trading iron and lead and copper for drugs with fantastic properties that were grown in Skaith's narrow tropic zone and for antiquities looted from the ruins of old cities. So the Wandsmen let them stay, and Skeg became a marketplace for the off-worlders.

But the ships brought with them more than iron pigs. They brought hope. And that hope was a corrupting influence.

It led some folk to think of freedom.

The people of Irnan, a city-state in the north temperate zone, had thought of freedom so strongly that they asked the Galactic Union, through its consul, to help them emigrate to a better world. And that precipitated the crisis. The Wandsmen reacted furiously to dam this first small trickle, which they foresaw would turn into a flood as other city-states saw the possibilities of escape. They took Ashton, who had come out

13

from Pax as representative of the Ministry of Planetary Affairs to confer with the Irnanese, and sent him north to the Citadel for the Lords Protector to question and deal with. With his ready-made mob of Farers, Gelmar, Chief Wandsman of Skeg, shut down the GU consulate and made Skeg a closed enclave which no foreigner might leave. Other Wandsmen, under Mordach, punished the Irnanese, making them prisoners in their own city. And when Stark came to find Ashton, the Wandsmen were waiting for him.

Gerrith, wise woman of Irnan, had prophesied that a Dark Man would come from the stars. A wolf's-head, a landless man, a man without a tribe. He would destroy the Citadel and the Lords Protector for the sake of Ashton.

For that prophecy the wise woman died, and Stark came very near to dying. He fitted the description. A mercenary, he owned no master. A wanderer of the space-roads, he had no land of his own. Orphaned on an alien world, he had no people. Gelmar and his Farers had done their best to kill him at Skeg before he could begin his search. Word of the prophecy had been carried far and wide among the scattered peoples of Skaith. It had dogged Stark all the way north, so that he was alternately considered a savior to be worshipped and encumbered, a blasphemy to be destroyed out of hand and an article of value to be sold to the highest bidder. The prophecy had not in any way helped him.

Nevertheless, he had managed to do what the prophecy had said he would do. He had taken the Citadel and gutted it with fire. Because of the Northhounds and their inbred loyalty, he had not been able to kill the Lords Protector. But they would be destroyed in another sense when it became known to the people that they were not at all supernatural beings, undying and unchanging, but only seven Wandsmen who had achieved the positions of supreme authority for ordering the affairs of the Fertile Belt—seven old men cast out now upon the world by no greater power than that of an off-planet adventurer.

So far, so good. But the wise woman had not said what would follow the fulfillment of her prophecy.

Of the six who had left Irnan to find the Citadel, only three survived: Stark himself; Gerrith the daughter of Gerrith, who had become the wise woman in her mother's place; and Halk, that strong man and slayer of Wandsmen, comrade of the martyred Yarrod. The rest had died when the men of Thyra took Stark and the others captive for Gelmar. Thanks to Gerrith and the interference of Kell à Marg Skaith-Daughter, who had insisted that Gelmar bring the strangers into the House of the Mother so that she might learn the truth of the rumored starships, Stark had escaped from the Wandsman. He had almost died in the dark catacombs under the Witchfires, in endless rooms and corridors long abandoned and forgotten by the Children of Skaith themselves. But he had at last made his way out by the north gate, to face the Northhounds and take the Citadel.

Gelmar still held Halk and Gerrith and was hurrying them south to be displayed before the walls of Irnan as evidence of the failure and folly of the revolt which had flared so suddenly into bloody violence. Irnan still stood against the anger of the Wandsmen, defying siege, hoping for allies and waiting for word from the north. When it became known that the Citadel had truly fallen, that the Lords Protector were human and vulnerable even as other men, then other city-states would be encouraged to join with Irnan in striking out for the freedom of the stars.

Stark knew that he could count on the Lords Protector and the Wandsmen to do everything in their power to stop him. And their power was enormous. Here in the thinly populated north they maintained it by bribery and diplomacy rather than by strength. But in the Fertile Belt, the green girdle that circled the old planet's middle zones and contained the bulk of her surviving peoples, their power was based on long tradition and on the mob rule of the Farers, those wayward charges of the Lords Protector who lived only for joy beneath their dying sun. Where necessary, the

Wandsmen also employed well-armed and disciplined mercenary troops such as the Izvandians. The farther south Stark went, the more formidable his enemies would become.

Stark's mount was beginning to give out. He was just too big for it. Ashton's was in better case, having less to carry. In spite of his years Ashton retained the rawhide leanness Stark remembered from the beginning, the same tough alertness of eye and mind and body. Even after numerous promotions had landed him in a soft job with the Ministry of Planetary Affairs, Ashton had refused to become deskbound. He continued stubbornly to do his researches into planetary problems in the field, which was why he had come to Skaith and run himself head-on into the Wandsmen.

At least, Stark thought, he had gotten Ashton out of the Citadel alive and safe. If he did not get him back to Skeg and off-planet the same way, it would not be for lack of trying.

The wind blew stronger. The sand moved under it with a dreary restlessness. The hounds trotted patiently: Gerd, who would have been king-dog after Flay; Grith, the great grim bitch who was his mate; and the seven other survivors of the attack on the Citadel— hellhounds with deadly eyes and their own secret way of killing. Old Sun seemed to pause on the rim of the mountain wall as if to rest and gather strength for the final plunge. In spite of himself, Stark felt a passing fear that this descent might be the last one and that the ginger star might never rise again, a common phobia among Skaithians which he seemed to be acquiring. Shadows collected in the hollows of the desert. The air turned colder.

Gerd said abruptly, *Things coming.*

4

The hound had stopped in his trotting. He stood braced on forelegs like tree trunks, high shoulders hunched against the wind, coarse fur ruffling. His head, which seemed too heavy for even that powerful neck to support without weariness, swung slowly back and forth. The dark muzzle snarled.

The pack gathered behind him. They were excited, making noises in their throats. Their eyes glowed, too bright, too knowing—the harbingers of death.

There, said Gerd.

Stark saw them, strung along a rib of sand in the grainy light. A second before nothing had stood there. Now, in the flicker of an eyelid, there were eleven . . . no, fourteen bent, elongated shapes, barely recognizable as human. Skin like old leather, thick and tough, covered their staring bones, impervious to wind and cold. Long hair and scanty scraps of hide flapped wildly. A family group, Stark thought—males, females, young. One of the females clutched something between pendulous breasts. Other adults carried stones or thighbones.

"Runners," Ashton said, and pulled out his sword. "They're like piranha fish. Once they get their teeth in—"

The old male screamed, one high wild cry. The ragged figures stooped forward, lifted on their long legs and rushed out across the shadowed sand.

They moved with incredible speed. Their bodies were drawn and thinned for running, thrusting heads carried level with the ground and never losing sight of the prey. The upper torso was all ribcage, deep and narrow, with negligible shoulders, the arms carried like

17

flightless wings outstretched for balance. The incredible legs lifted, stretched, spurned, lifted, with a grotesque perfection of motion that caught the throat with its loveliness even as it terrified with its ferocity.

Gerd said, *N'Chaka. Kill?*

Kill!

The hounds sent fear.

That was how they killed. Not with fang or claw. With fear. Cold cruel deadly mind-bolts of it that struck like arrows to the brain, drained the gut, chilled the blood-warm heart until it ceased beating.

The Runners were like birds before the hunters when the guns go off.

They dropped, flailing, writhing, howling. And the Northhounds went playfully among them.

Ashton still held the unnecessary sword. He stared at the pack with open horror.

"No wonder the Citadel remained inviolate for so long." His gaze shifted to Stark. "You survived *that?*"

"Barely." Once again he was back on the nighted plain, with the snow beneath him and the bitter stars above, and Flay's great jaws laughing while he sent the killing fear. "I almost went under. Then I remembered being afraid before, when Old One was teaching me to live in that place where you found me. I remembered the rock lizards hunting me, things as big as dragons, with bigger teeth than Flay. It made me angry that I should die because of a hound. I fought back. They're not invincible, Simon, unless you think they are."

The hounds were snapping the grotesque bodies back and forth like rags, playing toss and tug-of-war. Stark caught a glimpse of the female with the hanging breasts. What she had clutched between them was an infant, its tiny browless face snarling savagely even in death.

"There are some worse than that in the darklands on the other side of the mountains," Stark said, "but not much worse." Scraps and remnants of old populations left behind by the Great Migrations had solved the

18

problems of survival in numerous ways, none of them pleasant.

"The Hooded Men hate and fear the Runners," Ashton said. "They used to range much farther north, but now they're in bitter competition for what few resources are left in this wilderness. They can run down anything that moves, and anything that moves is food: humans, domestic animals, anything. The weaker tribes are suffering the most, the so-called Lesser Hearths of the Seven Hearths of Kheb. They've taken to raiding south, all the way to the cliff villages below Yurunna, along the Edge. The Ochar, who call themselves the First-Come, fare much better because of the supplies they get from the Wandsmen. The Lesser Hearths do not love them. There is war between them and between each other. And the Ochar will not love you, Eric. They're hereditary Keepers of the Upper Road, and their existence depends on the Wandsmen. With the Citadel gone and no more traffic between it and Yurunna . . ." He made an expressive gesture.

"So far," said Stark, "I've found very few on Skaith to love me."

Only one, in fact.

Her name was Gerrith.

When the hounds were done with their gamboling and their crunching, Stark called them to heel.

They came reluctantly. *Good play, full belly,* Gerd said. *Now sleep.*

Later sleep, Stark answered, and looked into the bright baleful eyes until they slid aside. *Now hurry.*

They hurried.

The last dull glow faded. Stars burned in the desert sky, dimmed intermittently by the flaring aurora. Skaith has no moon, and the Three Ladies, the magnificent clusters that ornament the more southerly nights, gave no light here. Nevertheless, it was possible to follow the markers.

The wind dropped. The cold deepened. Warm breath steamed white, froze on the faces of the men and the muzzles of the beasts.

19

Gerd said, *Wandsmen. There.*

The hounds could not distinguish between the different grades of Wandsmen, except that Gerd pictured *white* in his mind, which was the color of the robes worn by the Lords Protector.

Presently Stark made out a trampled track in the sand, and he knew that they were very close.

The riding animals had begun to stagger with weariness. Stark called a halt. They fed and rested and slept a while. Then they went on their way again, following the broad trail over the dunes.

The first coppery smudge of dawn showed in the east. It widened slowly, dimming the stars, staining the land like creeping rust. The rim of the ginger star crawled up over the horizon. And from somewhere ahead, Stark heard voices chanting.

"Old Sun, we thank thee for this day. For light and warmth we thank thee, for they conquer night and death. Abandon not thy children, but give us many days in which to worship thee. We worship thee with gifts, with precious blood . . ."

From the top of a dune Stark looked down and saw the camp: a score of servants, a huddle of beasts and baggage and, some distance apart by the remains of a fire, the seven old men—the Lords Protector, their rich robes of fur over white garments, offering the morning prayer. Ferdias was pouring wine onto the last of the embers.

He looked up at the Northhounds and at the two Earthmen on the back of the dune. Stark saw his face clearly, a strong face, proud and implacable. The dawn wind stirred his robes and his mane of white hair, and his eyes were as cold as winter ice. His companions, six dark pillars of rectitude, looked up also.

The chant did not waver. ". . . with precious blood, with wine and fire, with all the holy things of life. . ."

Wine hissed into the hot ashes, steaming.

And Gerd whined.

What is it? Stark asked.

Not know, N'Chaka. Wandsmen angry. Gerd lifted

20

his head, and his eyes caught the light of Old Sun so that they burned like coals.

Wandsmen want to kill.

5

Very quietly Stark said to Ashton, "Don't make any threatening moves. Stay close to me."

Ashton nodded, looking uneasily at the nine gaunt giants who stood almost as tall as the riding animals. He settled himself in the saddle and took a firmer grip on the rein.

Stark forgot him for the moment.

The Northhounds were incapable of understanding the complexities of their betrayal. According to pack law, they had followed a new leader, one who had established beyond doubt his right to lead. They had followed him to the Citadel; and the servants, the Yur, to whom they owed no loyalty, had attacked them with arrows. They did not understand why. They only understood the wounds, and their rage had been deadly. But they had offered no threat of harm to the Wandsmen, the Lords Protector. They had forbidden N'Chaka to touch them. As they saw it, they had been loyal to their trust. They were to prevent all humans from reaching the Citadel, but they did not regard N'Chaka as human. They saw nothing wrong in allowing him to go there.

Yet, when Ferdias ordered Gerd to kill N'Chaka in the Citadel, Gerd had wavered dangerously. Only the knowledge of what N'Chaka had done to Flay decided the outcome.

Now there would be another test.

Stark thought of Flay, of the death of Flay, torn and

bleeding on the plain. He made the thoughts strong. And he said:

Watch the servants. They may send more arrows to us.

Gerd's lips pulled back. He growled. The gash across his own hip was still raw and painful.

We watch.

Stark kicked his beast into a walk, down the slope of sand toward the Lords Protector. Ashton followed. The hounds padded beside Stark, carrying their heads low, snarling.

The Yur remained motionless, staring at the pack with their shining copper-colored eyes that were like the inlaid eyes of statues, reflecting light but no depth. Their faces were beautiful to see, but so alike that they were all the same face, a face totally lacking in expression. Yet Stark could smell the fear, the rank sweat of it upon them. They had not forgotten what the Northhounds had done to their brothers.

Old Sun had completed his rising. Ferdias poured out the last of the wine. The chanting stopped. The seven old men waited by the ashes of the fire.

The Earthmen and the hounds reached the bottom of the slope and halted before the Lords Protector. Stark slid off the saddle-pad, coming to the ground with the easy grace of a leopard.

"We will have six of your beasts, Ferdias," he said. "The best and strongest. Have your servants bring them now, but bid them take care." He put his hand on Gerd's high shoulders.

Ferdias inclined his head slightly and gave the order.

Nervous activity began among the Yur. Ashton dismounted carefully. They waited.

The Lords Protector looked at the Earthmen as at two incarnate blasphemies.

Especially they looked at Stark.

Seven iron men, they were believers in a creed and a way of life, the only ones they knew. Skaith was their world, Skaith's peoples their people. They had served all their lives to the best of their considerable abilities, honoring the ancient law—succor the weak, feed the hungry, shelter the homeless, strive always for the greatest good of the greatest number.

They were good men. Not even Stark could question their goodness.

He could question the lengths to which that goodness had been carried. Lengths that had made the blood-bath at Irnan inevitable and had brought about the deaths of equally good men and women who wanted the freedom to choose their own path among the stars.

Despite his hatred, Stark felt a certain sympathy for the Lords Protector. A little more than a decade was hardly time enough in which to absorb the enormous implications of what had happened. Skaith's little sky had been a tight-closed shell for all the ages of its existence. Uncounted generations had lived and died within that shell, seeing nothing beyond. Now, with a single dagger-stroke, that sky was torn open and Skaith stared out upon the galaxy—stunning in its immensity, thronged with unimagined worlds and peoples, ablaze with the glare of alien suns, busy with life where Skaith was concerned only with her long dying.

Small wonder that new thoughts were stirring. And small wonder that these well-nigh all-powerful men were desperately afraid of what the future might hold. If Irnan succeeded in her revolt, and other stable populations, those who supplied the food and commodities to support the vast army of Farers, should join with her in emigrating to freer worlds, all the dependants of the Lords Protector would be left destitute and the whole order would be destroyed.

"It is not right or decent," said Ferdias slowly, "that any creature in human form should control the North-hounds on their own level, as a beast."

"He will not control them long," said a small lean man with intense black eyes. "They cannot live where Old Sun is stronger."

"That is true," said Ferdias. "They are bred for the cold north."

Stark shrugged. He was not worried about that day. He was worried about this one. Gerd moved uneasily,

23

and Stark let his hand slide down to the hound's broad head.

"Why do we not kill this person here at once?" said the black-eyed man. "The hounds will not touch us."

"Can you be sure?" said Ferdias. "We have never killed a Northhound, and they regard him as one of their own."

"Besides," said Stark, "I'd set them on the Yur. Then you'd be alone, at the mercy of the Runners, the bellies without minds. Even the Lords Protector are not safe from them."

Another one of the six spoke up, a tall gaunt man whose wild hair was blowing across his face. His eyes glared out through it as from a thicket. He shouted at Stark.

"You cannot hope to live. You cannot hope to see Irnan again or the ships at Skeg."

Ferdias said, "I think it is useless to argue with Stark that he has no hope of doing whatever it is he intends to do. This was argued when he determined to fulfill the prophecy of Irnan."

"A prophecy of traitors!" cried the wild-haired man. "Very well, he has fulfilled it. He has taken back the man Ashton and burned our sacred roof over our heads. But that is the end of the prophecy, and the end of the Dark Man. He is no more fated."

"Unless there should be another prophecy," said Ferdias, and smiled without the slightest warmth or mirth. "But that is hardly likely. Gerrith goes to her own fate. And by her words, since Mordach destroyed the Robe and Crown, there is no longer a wise woman for Irnan."

"Wise woman or not," said Ashton, "and prophecies be damned, the change will come. Skaith herself will force it on you. The change can be peaceful, controlled by you, or it can be hideously violent. If you have the wisdom and the foresight to bring Skaith into the Union—"

Ferdias said, "We have listened to you for many months, Ashton. Our opinions have not been altered, not even by the fall of the Citadel." His gaze dwelt again on Stark, and the hounds muttered and whined and were restless. "You hope to destroy us by revealing to the world that we are not immortals but only men, only Wandsmen grown older. Perhaps this may come about. It has not happened yet. The Harsenyi nomads will carry the tale of the Citadel's fall in their wanderings, but it will be a long time in the telling. No doubt you sent messengers of your own, or tried to, to take word swiftly to Irnan. Messengers can be intercepted. Irnan is under siege. We hold all the Fertile Belt. We hold Skeg, your only hope of escape, and the starport is under guard at all times—you can hardly hope to reach it without being captured. And Skaith herself is your enemy. She is a cruel mother, but she is ours, and we know her. You do not."

He turned abruptly. "The beasts are ready. Take them and go."

Stark and Ashton mounted.

Ferdias spoke aloud to Gerd, so that Stark too might hear him. "Go now with N'Chaka. You will come back to us when it is time."

The Earthmen rode out of the camp with the hounds behind them.

They rode for some distance. The camp was lost behind them in the dunes.

Stark's muscles relaxed as the adrenaline stopped flowing. Sweat broke out on him, clammy beneath his furs. Ashton's face was a study in hard-drawn lines. Neither man spoke. Then at last Ashton sighed and shook his head and said softly, "Christ! I thought surely they'd try to turn the brutes against us."

"They were afraid to," Stark said. "But there will be another time."

The hounds trotted peacefully.

"It seems such a primitive idea," Ashton said, "setting them to guard the Citadel."

"That's what they wanted. The Lords Protector had men-at-arms in plenty to defend them during the Wandering, but men will face other men and weapons they can see. The great white hounds appearing suddenly out of the snow—wraiths with demon eyes and a supernatural power to kill—was something most men preferred to avoid, and of course the ones who didn't, died. In time the legend became even more effective than the fact."

"The Lords Protector must have killed many people who only wanted help."

"The Lords Protector have always been realists. The important thing was that the Citadel should remain sacrosanct, a mystery and a power hidden from men. A few lives had to be sacrificed for the good of the many." Stark's face hardened. "You weren't at Irnan, Simon, tied to a post, waiting to be flayed alive by the will of Mordach, the Chief Wandsman. You didn't hear the mob howl, you didn't smell the blood when Yarrod was slaughtered and torn."

Gerrith did. Gerrith was there, stripped naked but not shamed before the mob, defying Mordach, calling out to the people of Irnan in the clear strong voice of prophecy. *Irnan is finished here on Skaith, you must build a new city, on a new world, out among the stars.* She had waited there for death, beside him. As had Halk, and those three who had died at Thyra trying to reach the Citadel.

Ashton had his own bitter memories of captivity and threatened death. He was only alive himself because the Lords Protector had not quite dared to be deprived of his knowledge of this new and unknown foe they had to deal with—the vast Outside.

"I know how they think," he said. "But they're not being realists about the future. The viable surface of this planet gets smaller every year. The marginal peoples are already beginning to move as the cold drives them and the food supplies dwindle. The Lords Protector are perfectly aware of this. If they don't act in time, they'll have another slaughter on their hands, such as they had at the time of the Wandering."

"It was the slaughter that gave them their power," Stark said. "They can accept another one as long as they retain their power which they will never give up."

"We're asking them to do more than give up power.

We're asking them to cease being. Where does a Lord Protector go when he has nothing left to protect? They have meaning only in the existing context of Skaith. If we take away that context, they disappear."

"That," said Stark, "is the best fate I could ask for them."

He picked up the reins. The road markers marched away in the morning. Gelmar was somewhere ahead. With Gerrith.

The men made much better time now, changing mounts frequently. The pack load was shared between two led animals. The beasts were by no means fresh, but they were stronger than the ones that had been left behind. Stark pushed them without mercy.

Gelmar was pushing, too. Three times they came upon dead animals. Stark half-expected to find Halk's body left by the wayside. The man had taken a great wound at Thyra, and this pace would no doubt finish him.

"Perhaps Halk is dead," Ashton suggested, "and they're carrying the corpse. They can display him just as well, pickled in wine and honey."

The wind blew fitfully, veering with a kind of spiteful malice so that it could kick sand in their faces no matter how they turned them. Toward noon a haze came out of the north and spread across the sky. Old Sun sickened, and the face of the desert was troubled.

Ashton said, "The Runners often come with the sandstorms. In force."

They drove their mounts to the limit and beyond, passing each marker as an individual triumph. The beasts groaned as they went. The hounds ran with their jaws wide and their tongues lolling.

The haze thickened. The light of the ginger star yellowed and darkened. The wind struck at the men with vicious little cat's-paws. Sky, sun and desert lost definition, became merged into one strange brassy twilight.

In that distanceless and horizonless half-gloom Stark and Ashton came to the top of a ridge and saw Gelmar's party ahead, a line of dark figures clotted to-

27

gether, puffs of blowing sand rising beneath them as they moved.

6

Stark said to Gerd, *Run. Send fear to the servants if they fight. Hold them all until I come.*

Gerd called his pack together. They fled away, nine pale shadows. They bayed, and the terrible voices rang down the wind. The people of Gelmar's party heard and faltered in their going.

Stark handed his lead-reins to Ashton and flogged his beast into a lumbering gallop.

A spume of sand had begun to blow from the tops of the dunes. The wind was settling into the northeast quandrant. Stark lost the voices of the hounds. For a time he lost sight of the party, because of a dusty thickness in the lower air that came down like a curtain on the flat below the ridge. When he saw them again, blurred shapes of men and animals rubbed with a dark thumb on an ocher canvas, they were standing perfectly still. Only the hounds moved, circling.

Stark rode up to the group. The face he was looking for was not the first one he saw. That was Gelmar's. The Chief Wandsman of Skeg sat his mount a little apart from the others, as though perhaps he had turned to intercept the hounds. The strain of the journey showed on him and on the three other Wandsmen who accompanied him. Stark knew them all by sight but only one by name—that was Vasth, who had wrapped his ruined face in a scarf against the cold. Halk had struck him down at Irnan, on that day when the city rose and killed its Wandsmen. Vasth was apparently the only survivor. His remaining eye peered at Stark, a vicious glitter between the wrappings.

Gelmar had changed considerably since Stark first met him, tall and lordly in his red robe, secure in his unquestioned authority, ordering the mob at Skeg. The Wandsman had taken his initial shock that night, when Stark laid violent hands on his sacred person and made it clear to him that he could die as easily as any other man. He had received further shocks, all connected with Stark. Now he looked at the Earthman, not as would a superior being with power unlimited, but as a tired man, one who was exasperated, thwarted and quite humanly angry—seeing another defeat, but not beaten. Gelmar was not ever going to be beaten as long as he could breathe.

Gerd ranged himself at Stark's side. *Wandsmen angry we follow N'Chaka.*

Angry with N'Chaka. Not you.

Gerd whined. *Never angry at Flay.*

Flay is dead. Ferdias say follow me, for now.

Gerd subsided, unsatisfied.

Gelmar smiled briefly, having understood Gerd's side of the exchange. "You'll have difficulty holding them. They're not equipped to serve two masters."

"Would you care to put it to the test now?"

Gelmar shook his head. "No more than Ferdias did."

The Yur, ten or eleven of them scattered along the line, were standing quiet. Some were on foot, and they seemed less tired than the mounted Wandsmen. But they were bred for strength. They stared at the hounds with their blank bright eyes, and Stark thought they were puzzled rather than afraid. They knew what had happened at the Citadel, but they hadn't seen it. They were armed with bows and light lances, swords and daggers at their belts.

"The servants," Stark said, "will lay down their arms, very carefully. If any hostile move is made, the hounds will kill."

"Would you leave us at the mercy of the Runners?" cried one of the lesser Wandsmen.

"That concerns me not at all," said Stark. "You

have a dagger at your own waist. Discard it." He motioned to Gelmar. "Give the order."

"The hounds will not harm us," said Vasth. His voice came muffled through the scarf.

Gelmar said with cold impatience. "There is a sandstorm blowing. We need the Yur." To Stark he said, "The Runners come with the storms, living where other creatures would die. They come in strength, devouring everything in their path."

"So I have heard," said Stark. "Give the order."

Gelmar gave the order. The Yur dropped their weapons into the blowing sand. Gelmar loosened his own belt.

Stark kept his eyes on Vasth.

Gerd said, *Wandsman throw knife, kill N'Chaka.*

I know. Touch him, Gerd.

Not hurt Wandsman.

No hurt. Touch.

Gerd's baleful gaze turned to the Wandsman. Vasth was stricken with a sudden trembling. He made a strangled sound and let the dagger fall.

"Stand quiet now," said Stark, and called. "Gerrith!"

There was a covered litter slung between two animals. She came from beside it, shaking back the fur hood that covered her head. The wind picked up thick strands of hair the color of warm bronze. She smiled and spoke his name, and her eyes were like sunlight.

"Come here by me," he said.

She reined her beast to the side away from Gerd. Her face had been thinned by the long journeying, all the way from Irnan, across the Barrens and through the haunted darklands to the Citadel. The fine bones were clear under honed flesh and taut skin colored by the winds of Skaith to a darker bronze than her hair. Proud and splendid Gerrith. Stark was shaken by a stabbing warmth.

"I knew you were coming, Stark," she said. "I knew the Citadel had fallen, long before Ferdias' messenger reached us. But we must go on now, quickly."

"I have no mind to stay." The wind had strengthened, driving the sand. The weapons were already half-

30

buried. The world had become much smaller. The twilight had deepened so that even the faces of the Wandsmen and the Yur were indistinct. "Is Halk living?"

"Barely. He must have rest."

Ashton appeared dimly out of the murk with the led beasts. "Let them go, Simon," Stark said. "Gerrith, can you two handle the litter?"

They went at once and took the places of the two servants who had been leading the animals. Then they rejoined Stark.

"Gelmar. Tell your people to move."

The cavalcade moved, reluctantly, thinking of weapons left behind. Riders hunched in saddles, covered faces from stinging sand. Little drifts piled on Halk's litter.

They passed a marker, and Stark was squinting ahead trying to see the next one when Gerd said:

Humans. There.

Stark rode closer to Gelmar. "What humans? Hooded Men? The wayhouse?"

Gelmar nodded.

They went on.

When Stark reckoned they were far enough away from the buried weapons to make impractical any attempt to recover them, he reached out and caught Gelmar's bridle.

"We leave you here. Follow too closely and your servants die.

Kill Yur? Gerd asked hopefully.

Not unless I tell you.

"After you have secured the wayhouse," Gelmar said, "what then?"

"He will leave us to die in the sand," said Vasth. "May Old Sun shrivel the men from the stars!"

The cavalcade had halted, bungling together behind Gelmar.

"I would prefer to show you the same mercy you have shown us," said Stark. "But if you make it to the wayhouse, I'll not deny you shelter."

31

Gelmar smiled. "You could not. The hounds would force you to let us in."

"I know," said Stark. "Otherwise I might be less generous."

He rode away from the party, with Ashton and Gerrith and the litter.

Lead us to humans, he said to Gerd, knowing that Gelmar would be following the same mental beacon. They could forget about the markers.

They plunged on, across whaleback dunes that blurred and shifted shape beneath them. The litter swayed and jolted. Stark was sorry for Halk, but there was no help for it. The desert cried out in torment, a great hissing gritty wail rose and circled and fell away again to a deep moaning.

Then, abruptly, the wind dropped. The lower air cleared in the sudden stillness. Old Sun shone raggedly above. From the top of a ridge they saw the wayhouse half a mile or so ahead, a thick low structure of stone with a series of drift-walls about it to keep the desert out.

Ashton pointed away and said, "God Almighty."

A *tsunami,* a tidal wave of sand, rushed toward them out of the northeast. It filled the whole horizon. Its crest of dusty foam curled halfway up the sky. Below, it was a brightish ocher shading down through dirty reds and browns to a boiling darkness at the bottom that was almost black.

Stark saw a scudding of many shapes that ran fleetly before the edges of that blackness.

For the second time Gerd said, *Things come.*

Gelmar's party appeared on the back trail, clear in the placid air. They paused and looked northeastward, then came on again at a run.

Stark lashed the beasts forward. The wave had a voice, a roaring almost too deep for the human ear to register. The heart felt it, and the marrow of the bones, and the spasming gut. Even the animals forgot their weariness.

All at once Gerd spoke urgently in Stark's mind.

Wandsman says come, N'Chaka. Come now or things kill.

He turned with the pack and raced away down the back trail, answering Gelmar's call.

7

Stark said, *Gerd, come back!*

The hounds ran on.

Danger, N'Chaka. Guard Wandsmen. You come.

"What is it?" shouted Ashton, his voice a thin thread against the far-off roaring. "Where are they going?"

"To guard the Wandsmen." The overriding imperative, the instinct bred in the bone. And Gelmar's cry for help must have been urgent enough, what with his escort unarmed and the Runners coming. Stark swore. If he let the pack go without him, N'Chaka might never regain his authority. He could not make the hounds return to him. Neither could he afford to let Gelmar get control of them.

"I have to go with them." He waved the others on. "Get to the wayhouse, Simon." Gerrith's face, pale under the bronze, and framed in dark fur, stared at him. The litter careened wildly, the muffled form within it so still that Stark wondered if any life was left. "Go!" he yelled. "Go!" He reined his beast around and sent it staggering after the hounds, his thoughts as black as the base of the sand wave.

He met Gelmar's party in a space between two dunes. All the Yur were on foot now, running more strongly than the beasts. Two ran at the head of each Wandsman's mount, helping it along. The North-hounds hovered on the flanks.

Gelmar looked at Stark with a certain cruel amusement. "I wondered if you'd come."

33

Stark did not answer. He fell in at the head of the party, sword in hand. The crest of the wave, out-speeding the base, began to spread overhead. Dirty veils of grit trailed down from it. The air was thickening again. When they topped a dune, Stark could see the wall of sand sweeping nearer.

The Runners scudded before it as if riding a sand-storm gave them even more pleasure than sex or feeding. It was a game, such as Stark had seen strong-winged birds play with storm winds, and there was a sinister beauty in the flickering movement of bending shapes, a sort of dark dance, swift and doomsome. He could not count the creatures, but he guessed at half a hundred. Perhaps more.

They were not moving at random. They had a goal.

"The wayhouse?"

"There is food there. Men and animals."

"How do they attack?"

"With the stormfront. While their victims are stunned and suffocating, they feed. They survive the dust, and they seem to enjoy the violence. They strike like Strayer's Hammer."

Strayer was a god of the forges worshipped by certain iron-working folk on the other side of the mountains. Stark had had some experience of that hammer.

"We must have shelter," he said, "before the sand wave hits, or we'll be so scattered that even the hounds won't be able to help us."

From the next ridge Stark made out the smudged images of Ashton, Gerrith and the litter. They had reached the walls and begun to pass through a gate. Stark lost sight of them as he came sliding down to the flat. Flying grit blinded him. The ground shook. The huge solemn roaring filled the world.

Half a mile.

Seven and a half minutes walking. Half of that running flat out for your life.

Stay close, Gerd! Lead to humans!

Gerd's head pressed his knee. He felt the hound tremble.

No worse than snowblind storm on Worldheart. Lead, Gerd!

Grith came shouldering up beside her mate. *We lead.*

The air was a darkening turmoil. They fled across the face of the storm, toward the walls they could no longer see.

Things come, N'Chaka.

Kill?

Too far. Soon.

Hurry, then!

Wind plucked at them, trying to lift them into the sky. Stark counted seconds. At one hundred and seventy a wall loomed in the murk, so close that they almost came against it. The gate. The gate!

Here, N'Chaka.

An opening. They passed through it. Now that they were within the walls of the fury of the wind seemed to abate somewhat, or else there was a space of dead air just before the wave. They could see the squat stone house ahead, beyond an inner wall and forever out of reach. They could see, much closer to them, some long low pens for the sheltering of animals, roofed over and open to the south, empty.

They could see the wave burst over the northeast walls in great boiling spouts of sand, dun-colored against black.

The Runners came with the boiling sand spouts, skimming the ground with outstretched arms. They were filled with a demoniac energy, as though they drew strength from the dynamics of wind and erupting desert.

Stark dropped from the back of his foundering beast and caught tight hold of Gerd's coarse neck-fur with his left hand. The Yur were behind him, fairly carrying the Wandsmen, the hounds hanging close, shoulders jostling. The pens offered no security but they were shelter of a sort, better than the open. They flung themselves under the nearest roof, against the nearest wall.

The wave hit.

Black, roar, dust, cracking, shaking, world falling. The wind hated them for cheating it. The air beneath the roof was thick with sand, and the sand had faces in it, gargoyle faces, film-eyed and browless, with great snapping teeth.

Kill!

The hounds killed.

Part of the roof ripped away. Runners were there, kicking, tearing. Their strength was appalling. The hounds killed, but some of the Runners plummeted down through the holes, onto the prey beneath. The Yur had placed the Wandsmen in a corner and formed a human wall across their front. They had only their hands to fight with. Runner jaws clamped on the living flesh and did not let go.

Stark killed with a furious loathing, slashing at anything that moved in the blind dust. There was a foul stink. The screaming of the Runners in rage and hunger and deadly fear came thin and terrible through the storm.

The hounds killed until they were tired.

Too many, N'Chaka. Strong.

Kill, kill, or Wandsmen die!

He did not care if the Wandsmen died. He only wanted to live himself.

The hounds killed.

The last of the Runner pack went whimpering away after the passing storm, to seek easier prey. There were heaps of ugly bodies left behind. But the hounds were too weary for play. They sat and hung their heads and let their tongues loll.

N'Chaka, we thirst.

Spent and shaken, Stark stood staring at the pack.

"They have their limits," said Gelmar. His face was ashen. "Of course they have." One of the Yur was beside him. "Give him your sword." And again, impatiently, "Your sword, Stark! Unless you wish to do the thing yourself."

The Wandsmen were unharmed. Two of the Yur were dead. Three others had been torn beyond hope.

Runner corpses were still attached to them, blood dripping from obscene jaws.

Stark handed over his sword.

Quickly and efficiently the Yur gave each the mercy-stroke. The eyes of the victims watched without emotion and became only a shade less bright in the beautiful blank faces as death overtook them. The uninjured servants stood by impassively. When he was finished, the Yur wiped the blade and returned the sword to Stark.

And it had all happened in the space of a few minutes. The concentrated savagery of the attack had been shocking. Stark realized that Gelmar was looking at the Runner bodies with a sort of horrified fascination.

"Never seen them before?"

"Only from a distance. And never . . ." Gelmar seemed to hesitate over some inner thought. "Never so many."

"Each year they come in greater numbers, Lord."

It was a new voice, authoritative and strong. Stark saw that four men had appeared in the open side of the pen. They were little more than shadows in the blowing dust. Hooded cloaks of leather, dyed the color of bittersweet, whipped about tall lean bodies. Faces were hidden behind wrappings of cloth of the same color, all but the eyes, which were blue and piercing. The man who had spoken stood in the chief's place ahead of the others. Pendant upon his forehead, under the hood, was a dull orange stone set in gold, much scratched and worn.

"We saw you just before the storm struck, Lord, but we were not able to come."

He was staring, as they all were, at the bodies of the Runners.

"The Northhounds did this?"

Gelmar said, "Yes."

The Hooded Man made a sign in the air and muttered something, glancing sidelong at the great hounds. Then he straightened and spoke to Gelmar. But his cold gaze had turned to Stark.

"In the house are two men and a woman who came

37

just before you. The gray-headed man we saw before, when the Wandsmen brought him north some months ago. They admitted they had been your prisoners. They told us that this stranger leads the Northhounds, so that they no longer obey you, and that we must take orders from him. We know, of course, that this is a lie."

He tossed back his cloak to show a sword, short and wickedly curved, and a knife whose iron grip looped over the knuckles for striking and was set with cruel studs.

"How do you wish us to take this man, Lord—alive or dead?"

8

Gerd moved his head and growled, catching the man's thought.

N'Chaka?

Send fear. Him! Not kill.

Gerd's hellhound gaze fixed on this tall chief of the Ochar, First-Come of the Seven Hearths of Kheb, and crumpled him sobbing into the dust like a terror-stricken child. His companions were too astonished to move.

"No!" cried Gelmar. "Stop it, Gerd!"

The hound whined irritably. *N'Chaka?*

Stark dropped his sword and caught Gerd's head, both sides, by the skin of his jowls.

Wandsmen not threatened. N'Chaka is. Who do you follow?

Have it out now, Stark thought. Now. Or we're back where we started, all of us—Gerrith, myself, Simon, Halk—all prisoners of the Wandsmen.

He drew houndskin tight between his fingers, stared into hot hound eyes.

Send fear.

The Ochar chief gasped and groveled in the sand.

"No," said Gelmar, who came and put his hand on Gerd's shoulder. "I forbid you, Gerd. You belong to us, to the Wandsmen. Obey me."

The Ochar chief ceased to struggle. He continued to sob. The three other men had moved away from him, as if he had been suddenly bewitched and they feared to be caught by the same spell. They appeared bewildered, unable to believe what they saw.

Gerd made an almost human cry. *N'Chaka! Not know.* He was tired, and the fight had left him edgy and upset. The smell of blood was strong. He pulled against Stark's hands. He threw himself from side to side, and his claws tore the dust.

Stark held him. *Choose, Gerd. Whom do you follow?*

A dangerous light had begun to kindle in Gerd's eyes. Abruptly the hound stood still, quivering in every muscle.

Stark braced himself.

The pack, by custom, would not interfere. The matter was between himself and Gerd. But they would see to it that no one else interfered, in a physical sense. There would be no danger of a knife in the back.

"Kill, Gerd," said Gelmar, his hand on the hound's shoulder. "This man will lead you all to death."

And Stark said, *You cannot kill me, Gerd. Remember Flay.*

The bolt of fear struck him. It shriveled his brain and turned his bones to water. It set his heart pounding until it threatened to burst against his ribs. But he held his grip. And a fierce cry came from out of his deep past, *I am N'Chaka. I do not die.*

The fear kept on.

Stark's pale eyes changed. His mouth changed. A sound came from his throat. He was no longer seeing Gerd as Gerd. He was seeing older, faraway things, the Fear-Bringers—the eternal enemy with all his many

39

faces of dread, hunger, storm, quake, deadly night, deadlier day, the stalking hunter snuffling after heartblood.

All life is fear. You have never felt it, hound. Death never feels it. Hound, I will teach you fear.

His grip shifted suddenly to Gerd's throat, gathered loose skin on either side, gathered and twisted, twisted and gathered, until the hound began to strangle, and still his fingers worked, and he said:

Do you see, Gerd, how it feels to die?

N'Chaka . . . !

The fear stopped.

Gerd dropped down, jaws wide, muzzle drawn in a snarling rictus. He put his chin on the ground.

Follow . . . strongest.

Stark let go. He straightened up. His eyes were still strange, all the humanness gone out of them. Gelmar stepped back, as though retreating from something unclean.

But he said, "You will not always be the strongest, Stark. Human or beast, your flesh is vulnerable. One day it will bleed, and the hounds will tear you."

The Ochar chief had risen to his knees. He wept tears of rage and shame.

"Do not let me live," he said. "You have put disgrace upon me before my tribesmen."

Stark said, "There is no disgrace. Is one man stronger than all these?" He pointed to the Runner bodies.

The Ochar chief got slowly to his feet. "No. But just now you withstood."

"I am not of your world. No man born of Skaith can stand against the Northhounds. And lest your tribesmen think shame of you, I will show them the truth of that."

Gerd squatted on his haunches, stretching his neck and hacking. Stark called the pack and they came around him, eyes averted lest they should seem to challenge him.

He gave an order, and the three Ochar were smitten with a palsy. They opened their mouths beneath the

40

orange wrappings and cried out. They ran stumbling away.

"Now," said Stark to the chief, "we will go to the house. Gelmar, take your people. Walk ahead of us." To the Ochar he said, "How are you called?"

"Ekmal."

"Stay by me, Ekmal. And remember that the hounds hear your thoughts."

He ordered the hounds to watch but not to kill unless he told them to.

The Wandsmen went ahead, hating him. The Yur, beautiful and blank, walked with the Wandsmen. Ekmal walked beside Stark, his hands well away from his girdle and the sharp blades. The hounds came at Stark's heels. The wind still blew and the air was brown, but a man could move in it if he had to.

Men in cloaks of orange leather were bringing animals out of the house, where they had been taken for safety. The animals were tall, with long legs and wide paws splayed and furred for the sand. They stepped daintily. They were all colors, black and yellow and brown, barred and spotted. Their arched necks bore slender heads set with intelligent amber eyes.

The men leading them had met the three Ochar who were fleeing from the hounds. They stood shouting at each other with much gesticulating. Then they all turned and stared, and some of them reached for weapons.

Stark said, "Speak to them, Ekmal."

"Put down your arms!" Ekmal cried. "These demon dogs have killed a hundred Runners. Obey this man or he will set them on us."

The men muttered among themselves, but they took their hands from their hilts. Ekmal turned to Stark.

"What do you wish of us?"

"Water for the hounds. Have all your beasts brought out and fitted to carry us—myself and your three captives. Have food . . ."

"All the beasts? We cannot!"

"All the beasts. With food and water."

41

"But without beasts we're prisoned here!" Ekmal had the desert man's horror of being left afoot.

"Exactly," said Stark. "And so will the Wandsmen be, and the Lords Protector when they come, if they survived the storm."

Ekmal stopped. His eyes widened. "The Lords Protector? Coming here?"

Gelmar said, "This off-worlder has pulled down the Citadel, Ekmal. He has burned it, and the Lords Protector are cast out."

A stillness came over the Hooded Men. They stood stiff and stricken in the wind.

Ekmal wailed and lifted his hands to the sky. "The Dark Man has fulfilled the prophecy. He has destroyed the Citadel, and there will be no more keeping of the road above Yurunna. He has destroyed us, the hereditary Keepers, the First-Come of Kheb. Our wives and our sacred mothers, our tall sons and blue-eyed daughters, all will die. Our villages will disappear beneath the sands. Even the Fallarin will not remember us."

All the Hooded Men cried out. And from within the house came a new lamenting in the voices of women.

There was a shrill scream, and something fell with a clatter onto stone, beyond the open doorway.

He had a bow, N'Chaka. To send arrows.

"Wait!" said Gelmar in his strong far-carrying voice. "Do nothing now. The hounds will strike you down. But your day will come. The Lords Protector do not abandon their children. The Citadel will be rebuilt, and there are no more prophecies. Skaith is old and strong. No one man, not even a stranger from the stars, can prevail against her. Let him go now. He will find his death in her arms."

"May she bury him deep," said Ekmal. "May Old Sun shrivel his bowels. May Runners eat him."

Stark said, "Give the orders."

Ekmal gave them, shooting sharp words like darts through the cloth that hid his face. The men obeyed, but their eyes held death, or rather the hope of it, for Stark. There were eleven of them besides the chief.

They led out all the animals, to the number of eighteen.

Ekmal said, "The well is inside."

Watch, Gerd.

The stonework of the house was solid and very old. Endless chafing of wind and sand had eroded it in whorls and pits. The edges of the doorway were worn round. On either side of the door, the wall wandered off to enclose a straggle of connected buildings that rose here and there to a second low story. Window places had been blocked up. At one corner was a little tower with many openings, and Stark could hear from within it a dim murmuring, as of birds. The wooden doors that worked on a pivot stone were enormously heavy and sheathed in iron brought by Harsenyi traders from Thyra beyond the mountains. The metal, far more valuable than pure gold, was scratched and scarred by Runner claws.

Inside, the air was still and warm, with pungent odors of animals and smoke and cooked foods. The stable area was off to the right, beyond a partition. The four Harsenyi beasts were there, standing with their heads down and their flanks heaving. The well had two stone troughs, one for the stable and one for humans.

The main room was large and neatly kept, with a dung fire smoking on a raised hearth. Weapons were ranged ready to hand. There were hangings and trophies on the walls, along with ornaments, some of them so exotic that they must have been brought up from the south over the Wandsmen's Road. Bags of grain, jars of wine and oil and other stores were kept in walled enclosures. At the back, the large room opened into a series of passageways leading to other quarters. The Wandsmen, Stark was sure, would have apartments fitted with every comfort. All in all, it was a pleasant place to rest from the rigors of travel.

A group of women, some holding small children to them, was gathered just inside the door. They wore long bright-colored garments of wool, and they did not cover their faces, which were thin-featured and hand-

43

some and fiercely hostile. They were clustered about one woman who knelt on the floor comforting a boy of about eleven. He wore a woolen tunic with an orange girdle, and he had not yet hidden his face behind the man's veil. He was trembling, biting back his sobs, and when he saw Stark he reached out for the bow he had dropped on the stones.

"No!" said Ekmal, and snatched up the bow. He touched the boy's bright head. "This is my son Jofr. I beg you—"

"Water the hounds," said Stark.

The women drew aside to let him pass. They bore themselves proudly. Their tawny necks and arms sounded when they moved with the soft clacking together of metal and darkling stones. Jofr rose to his feet and stood staring until his mother pulled him back.

Halk's litter had been set down close to the fire. Gerrith knelt beside it holding a cup. Ashton stood by her. Both had been watching, taut as bowstrings, to see who came in. They must have known something of what had gone on outside, but they could not be sure until they saw Stark and knew that he had survived the Runners and was somehow still in control.

Halk was watching, too.

"Over there," Stark said to Gelmar. "Sit down and be quiet." The hounds were lapping out of the trough. Hate and the death wish were as strong in the air around him as the smoke.

Watch, Gerd!

We watch, N'Chaka.

Stark walked to the fire, and the blue eyes of the women cursed him. Weariness gnawed at him, a corrosion in his bones. "Is there wine?"

Gerrith poured from a clay jug and handed him the cup. Ashton's gaze moved uneasily from the Wandsmen to the Hooded Men who came and went with gear and provisions.

"We must go on now," Stark said. "I can't stay awake forever, and I dare not risk the hounds." He bent over the litter. "Halk?"

Halk looked up at him. A tall man, taller than

44

Stark, he lay under the furs like a withered tree. The bones of his face stuck out through folds of skin where the flesh had dropped away. His huge hands were stiff bunches of twigs bound with purple cords. But his eyes were as hard and bright and contentious as ever, and his bloodless lips still managed the old fleering smile.

"Dark Man."

Stark shook his head. "The Citadel is gone, so is the Dark Man. The prophecy is finished, and I am no more fated. This choice is yours, Halk. Will you go with us, or must we leave you here?"

"I'll go," said Halk. His voice came groaning and whispering out of his hollow chest like wind from a cave. "And I'll not die, neither. I've sworn before Old Sun's face that I'll live to make of you an offering to the shade of Breca."

Breca had been Halk's shieldmate, struck down in the battle with the Thyrans. Those iron men had given her splendid body to the cannibal Outdwellers, mutton for the spit. Halk might have borne her death, but not that. And he blamed the Dark Man of the prophecy for having led them all to disaster.

"When do you plan to make this offering?" Stark asked.

"On the day when you are no longer useful to Irnan. Until then I'll fight beside you, for the city's sake."

Stark nodded. "I'll remember." To Gerrith and Ashton he said, "Gather your belongings." He called to two of the Hooded Men and told them to carry Halk's litter outside.

The hounds came dripping and slobbering from the trough.

Gelmar said, "Stark. They will not follow you below Yurunna. Then you will be two men and a woman with a half-dead burden to bow your backs and only your six hands between you to fight with when the Yur come to take you." He turned suddenly to Gerrith. "Has the wise woman something to say?"

She stood frozen in the act of pulling up her hood. She had the look of a prophetess once more, her eyes at once seeing and not seeing, fixed on Gelmar, her lips open to form words.

Stark said her name sharply. She started. Then for a moment she seemed bemused, like one waking suddenly from sleep in a strange place. Stark put his hand on her shoulder, guiding her toward the door. He did not answer Gelmar. There was nothing to say, except that what would happen would happen; and that they all knew anyway.

They passed the women and children. Jofr stood straight, a small thing of prey already shaped for his world.

Gerrith stopped. "Take the boy," she said.

The women screamed like eagles. Ekmal came, one hand for the boy and one for his dagger. Gerd growled.

Stark said, "I will not."

"No harm will come to him," Gerrith said, and her voice rang like a far-off bell. "Take him, Stark, or Mother Skaith will bury us all."

Stark hesitated. Then reluctantly he reached out for the boy.

Gerd growled louder.

"You heard the wise woman," Stark said. "No harm will come to him. Do not make me use the hounds."

The boy's mother spoke, one word, the deadliest one she knew. Ekmal's hand hovered over his knife. The hounds growled.

Stark said, "Come."

Jofr looked at his father. "Must I?"

"It seems so."

"Very well," said Jofr, and smiled. "I am an Ochar."

He stepped forward alone to Stark's side.

They went out into the yard. The animals were ready, linked by leading lines, three of them saddled with the high desert saddles, covered in worked leather with designs of many colors tempered by sun and wind. The litter was suspended between two of the animals, and Halk was once more an inert bundle, his face hidden beneath the hood.

They mounted. Stark took Jofr before him in the

saddle. They rode away from the house, past the heaps of Runner bodies by the pens, past the gnawed and scattered bones of the Harsenyi beasts.

Ekmal and the Hooded Men stood watching them until they vanished beyond the walls. Then Ekmal went into the house and spoke to Gelmar.

"Lord, is it true that he and that other are not born of Skaith-Mother?"

"That is true."

Ekmal signed the air. "Then they are demons. They have taken my son, Lord. What must I do?"

Without hesitation Gelmar said, "Bring the Swift-wing."

Ekmal went along one of the tunnels of the house. The tower of murmuring birds lay to his right, but he did not go to it. They were base creatures, fit only for food. He turned to the left and climbed narrow steps to a high apartment with window slits that let in the light of Old Sun and the wind of the desert. There were hangings of faded crimson on the walls, and trophies of weapons and skulls. Some of the skulls were brittle and yellow with age, crumbling dustily at the rims of the jaws and eyeholes.

In the center of the room, on an iron perch, sat a creature that seemed itself to be all of iron and bronze, a martial armor of shining feathers. Even with the great wings closed it had a look of speed and power, one sharp clean stroke from the crown of its snaky head to the last of its tapered tail. One of these dwelt in the house of every chief among the Ochar. Fed from the chief's table, with its slender collar of gold, it was the badge and sign and pride of chieftainship, ranking equally with honor and before life, wife, mother or child.

"Swiftwing," said Ekmal. "Sky-piercer. Wind-rider. Lightning-brother."

The creature opened eyes like two red stars and looked at Ekmal. It opened its beak and cried out stridently the only word it knew:

"War!"

"Of course, war," said Ekmal, holding out his arm.

47

9

The beasts were fresh and strong, striding easily over the sand. The hounds trotted quietly. The wind continued to drop, diminishing the brownness of the air.

Stark rode like a thundercloud, one arm about the small ferocity of Jofr, who sat straight and unbending, his body yielding only to the motion of the beast.

Gerrith said, "You are angry about the boy."

"Yes," said Stark. "I am angry about the boy. And I'm angry about something else—the visions."

"Let the boy go," Ashton said. "He can find his way back easily enough."

Gerrith sighed. "Do that if you will. But none of us will ever see Yurunna."

Ashton turned and studied her face. He had known many peoples on many worlds. He had seen many things that he could neither believe nor disbelieve, and he had acknowledged his ignorance.

"What did you see," he asked, "before Eric woke you?"

"I saw Eric . . . Stark . . . in a strange place, a place of rocks. There were Hooded Men there, but their cloaks were of different colors, not the orange of the First-Come. They seemed to be hailing Stark, and someone . . . something . . . was performing a ritual with a knife. I saw blood . . ."

The boy had stiffened in the circle of Stark's arm.

"Whose blood?" Stark asked.

"Yours. But it seemed to be shed in promise, in propitiation." She looked at Jofr. "The boy was there. I saw upon his forehead that he was to be your guide. Without him you would not find the way."

"You're sure of this?" Ashton said.

"I'm sure of what I saw. That is all I can be sure of. Has Stark told you? My mother was Gerrith, the wise woman of Irnan. She prophesied in the fullness of power. I do not. My gift is small and fitful. It comes as it will. I see, and I do not see." She turned to Stark. "You are angry about visions! I'm sick of them. I'd prefer to go blundering ahead without sight, as you do, trusting nothing but my own hands and brain. Yet these windows open and I look through them, and I must tell what I see. Otherwise . . ." She shook her head violently. "All that time in the stone house, with those things clawing and screaming to get in at us, I kept seeing you being torn apart and I couldn't tell whether it was the true sight or only my own fear."

Ashton said, "I had the same vision. It was fear."

"The hounds passed a miracle," Stark said. He was watching the boy's bright head, which was poised now with a new alertness.

Gerrith shuddered. "They'll come again."

"Not in such numbers, and the hounds will watch."

"If there's another sandstorm," said Ashton, "let's pray there's somewhere to hide. The next wayhouse is a week's journey."

"You'll not reach it," Jofr said. "My father will send the Swiftwing."

"Swiftwing?"

"The bird of war. All the clans of the Ochar will gather. Your demon dogs will kill many, no doubt, but there will be many more." He twisted around and smiled at Stark, his small white teeth showing sharp as a knife-edge.

"Um," said Stark. "And what of this place of rocks, and the Hooded Men who are not of the First-Come?"

"Ask the wise woman," said Jofr contemptuously. "It is her vision."

"Your father mentioned the Fallarin. Who are they?"

"I am only a child," said Jofr. "These things are not known to me."

Stark let it go. "Simon?"

"They're a winged folk," said Gerrith suddenly.

49

Ashton glanced at her. "Yes. Undoubtedly a controlled mutation like the Children of the Sea and the Children of Skaith. They seem to be held in some sort of superstitious awe by the Hooded Men. They are important to tribal life but in what way I was never told. The Ochar are closemouthed with strangers, and the Wandsmen respect their tabus. Anyhow, I had other things to think about. But I do know one thing, Eric."

"What?"

"When that boy said *I am an Ochar*, he was doing more than stating a fact or making an affirmation of courage. He was also saying that an Ochar knows the ways of the desert, sharing its powers; that an Ochar destroys his enemies, never turning aside from sacred feud as long as he has breath. That's a blue-eyed viper you hold there, and never forget it."

"I've known desert men before," said Stark. "Now let me think."

The wind dropped. The face of the desert became peaceful. The veils of dust fell away from Old Sun, and the rusty daylight showed the markers of the Wandsmen's Road marching on ahead, never so far apart that if one was buried the next one, or the one beyond that, could not be seen.

Stark said, "Simon, what lies beyond Yurunna? You spoke of something called the Edge."

"The plateau we stand on drops away, four thousand feet or so. It's much warmer below, and there are places where springs make cultivation possible. There are cliff villages—"

"Where the Hooded Men raid?"

"Not the villages themselves, they're out of reach, but they try to catch people in the fields, or steal their harvest. Beyond that is more desert until you come to the Fertile Belt."

"The good green land of the Farers."

"I was brought straight up the road from Skeg, so I didn't see too much of the country. The only city I saw was Ged Darod, the city of the Wandsmen. It was quite a place."

"A place of pilgrimage," Gerrith said. "Sanctuary, whorehouse, foundling home, spawning ground of more Wandsmen. That's where they're trained and taught, and every scrap of windblown rubbish in the world that drops there is made welcome."

"The whole of the lower city is crammed with Farers and pilgrims from all over Skaith. There are pleasure gardens—"

"I've heard of it," Stark said. "But first comes Yurunna."

Happy as a bird, Jofr's clear voice said, "You will not reach Yurunna."

He flung his arm skyward, a gesture of triumph. Where he pointed, high up, a winged shape of bronze and iron glinted and was quickly gone.

"It will go first to the nearest clan chiefs, and then to the farther ones. From its collar they will know that it belongs to my father. They will raise up their men at once, to come to him. You cannot pass through them on the way to Yurunna."

"Then we must go another way," said Stark. "And if there's no safety for us among the Ochar, we'll have to seek it among their enemies. Perhaps Gerrith's vision has purpose after all."

Ashton said, "You'll go to the Lesser Hearths?"

"It seems the only choice."

Jofr laughed. "The Ochar will still come after you. And the folk of the Lesser Hearths will eat you."

"Perhaps. What about you?"

"I am of the blood. I am man, not meat."

"What will they do to you?"

"I am a chief's son. My father will buy me back."

"Then will you guide us to the Lesser Hearths? Or at least to the nearest one."

"Gladly," said Jofr. "And I myself will share in the feasting."

Stark said to Gerrith, "This guide you have chosen for me does not inspire trust."

"I did not choose him," Gerrith snapped. "And I did not say he would guide you out of love."

"Which way?" asked Stark of Jofr.

51

Jofr considered. "The Hearth of Hann is nearest." He indicated a northeasterly direction, frowning. "I must wait for the stars."

"Does that sound right to you, Simon?"

Ashton shrugged. "Judging from where the Ochar lands are. They have the best, of course."

"The Lesser Hearths are weak," said Jofr. "The Runners eat them. When they are gone, we shall have all the land and water."

"But that time is not yet," said Stark. "Let's go."

They left the markers of the road behind them.

They moved on across boundless desolation while Old Sun slid down to the mountaintops and vanished in a cold brassy glare that streaked the land and then gave way to blackness and starshine and the dancing aurora.

Jofr studied the sky. "There. Where the big white one hangs under a chain of three. That is the way we must go."

They altered course toward the star.

"Have you been this way before?" asked Ashton.

"No," said Jofr. "But every Ochar knows the way to the hearths of his enemies. The Hearth of Hann is five days' journey. The Hann wear purple cloaks." He said it as though "purple cloaks" was a scatological term.

Stark said, "Do you know the name of that star?"

"Of course. It is Ennaker."

"The folk who live on its third world call it Fregor. Those who live on the fourth world call it Chunt. The folk of the fifth world also have a name, but I cannot shape their speech with my mouth. All the names mean sun."

Jofr set his jaw. "I do not believe you. There is only one sun, ours. The stars are lamps he has set to guide us."

"All those lamps are suns. Many of them have planets, and many of the planets support life. Did you think that Skaith was all alone, and you the only people in the universe?"

"Yes," said Jofr passionately. "That is the way it

must be. There have been stories about flaming eggs that fall from the sky and hatch demons in the form of men, but they are not true. My mother said they were only idle tales and not to be listened to."

Stark bent his head above Jofr, dark and grim in the night. "But I am a demon, boy, out of a flaming egg."

Jofr's eyes widened, reflecting the starlight. He caught his breath sharply, and his body seemed to shrink within the circle of Stark's arm.

"I do not believe," he whispered. He turned his face away and rode huddled and silent until they made camp.

Halk was still alive. Gerrith fed him wine and broth, and he ate and laughed at Stark. "Take a dagger to me, Dark Man. Else I shall live, as I told you."

They tied Jofr as comfortably as possible. Stark set the hounds to watch and said good night to Ashton, who looked up at him with a sudden unexpected grin.

"I'll tell you true, Eric. I don't think we'll make it, and I don't think I'll ever see Pax again; but it's good to get back to the old ways. I never was much for office work."

Stark said, "We'll fill you up with the other kind." He put his hand on Ashton's shoulder, remembering other nights by other fires on other worlds a long time ago. Ashton had learned about the pacific administration of wild worlds by doing, and Stark had gained his early knowledge of tactics and the art of dealing with all manner of peoples from his growing-up years with Ashton along the frontiers of civilization.

"Set your superior mind to work, Simon, and tell me: how do three men and a woman and a pack of hounds take over a planet?"

"I'll sleep on it," Ashton said, and did.

Stark went and stood by the fire. Halk was asleep. Jofr lay curled in his furs with his eyes shut. Gerrith sat watching the smoke rise from the glowing embers. She stood up and looked at Stark, and they went away a little from the fire, taking their furs with them. Gerd and Grith roused and followed. When they lay down together, the two hounds lay beside them.

There were many things to be said between them, but this was not a time for words. This was the coming together after separation, after captivity and the fear of death. They did not waste life in talking. Afterward they slept in each other's arms and were happy, and did not question the future. The deep-shared warmth of being was enough, for as long as they could have it.

On the second day after leaving the Wandsmen's Road, the character of the desert began to change. Underlying ridges rose up and became hills. The restless dunes gave place to eroded plains gashed with old dry riverbeds. Stark and his people rode through a haunted land.

There had been cities here. Not so many as in the darklands, which had been rich and fertile in their day, nor so large, but cities nonetheless, and their bones still lay along the riverbanks. Runners nested in them. Jofr seemed to have an instinct for cities. He seemed almost to smell them on the wind. But he said it was only that every Ochar boy was made to memorize the ancestral maps as well as the star-guides, so that no Ochar could ever be lost in the desert no matter what befell him. Stark tried to make him draw a map in the sand. He refused. Maps were tabu except for the Ochar.

The boy had been given a beast of his own to ride, and not the swiftest. He appeared to be content to lead. Stark trusted him not at all but he was not afraid. Gerd would tell him when the boy's mind contemplated treachery.

In the meantime Stark brooded, riding long hours without speaking, and then talking far into the night with Ashton and sometimes with Gerrith and Halk. It was after all their world.

Twice they waited until dark to skirt the ruins of a city, because the Runners did not hunt by night. At other times they saw roving bands of the creatures, but the hounds killed them or drove them off. And on a morning, suddenly, when they had been no more than two hours on the way and Old Sun was barely above the horizon, Gerd said:

N'Chaka. Boy think death.

At the same moment Jofr made an excuse to dismount and go apart. "Go straight on," he said. "I'll follow in a moment."

Stark looked ahead. There was nothing but a flat place of sand between two low ridges, and nothing unusual about the sand except that it was perfectly smooth and the color perhaps a shade lighter than the surrounding desert.

Stark said, "Wait."

The party halted. Jofr paused in the act of hiking up his tunic. Gerd came and stood beside him, dropping his huge jaw onto the boy's shoulder. Jofr did not move.

Stark dismounted and climbed one of the ridges. He picked up a large flat stone and threw it out onto the smooth sand.

The stone sank gently and was gone.

Gerd said, *Kill, N'Chaka?*

No.

Stark came back and looked at Gerrith, and Gerrith smiled. "I told you Mother Skaith would bury us all if you didn't take the boy."

Stark grunted. Much subdued, Jofr mounted again. They went around the sinking sand, and after that Stark kept an eye out for smooth places.

He knew that they were entering the territory of the Hann when they came upon the remains of a village. There had been wells and cultivation not so long ago. Now the small beehive houses were broken and gutted by the wind, and there were bones everywhere. Bones crushed and snapped and fragmented until there was no telling what sort of flesh they had once supported. The sand was full of gray-white chips.

"Runners," Jofr said, and shrugged.

"Surely the Runners attack Ochar villages," said Ashton. "How will your people hold all this land when you take it?"

"We're strong," said Jofr. "And the Wandsmen help us."

They passed two more villages, dead and disemboweled.

Beyond the third one, in midafternoon of the fifth day, with Halk propped up in his litter wide-awake, they saw ahead of them, on the top of a hill, a knot of riders in dusty purple.

Jofr whipped his beast forward, his voice screaming high and thin.

"Slay these men! Slay them! They are demons, come to steal our world!"

10

Stark said to the others, "Wait." He went forward slowly. Gerd paced at his right knee. Grith trotted out of the pack and came on his left. The seven other hounds came behind him. He rode with his right hand high and his left holding the rein well away from his body. Up on the hill one of the men snatched the yelling boy from his beast.

Stark went half of the distance between them and stopped. He counted eight purple cloaks. They did not move for a long while, except that the man who held Jofr cuffed him once, hard. The hounds sat in the sand and lolled their tongues, and no one reached for a weapon.

They know us, N'Chaka. They fear us.

Watch.

One of the men on the hill picked up his rein and moved down the slope.

Stark waited until the man halted before him. He was much like Ekmal, sinewy and blue-eyed, sitting his tall beast with the limber grace of the desert man whose life is made up of distances. His face was covered. The pendant stone on his brow that marked him a chief was a lighter purple than his leather cloak.

Stark said, "May Old Sun give you light and warmth."

"You are in the country of the Hann," said the chief. "What do you want here?"

"I wish to talk."

The chief looked from Stark to the Northhounds and back again.

"These are the deathhounds of the Wandsmen?"

"Yes."

"They obey you?"

"Yes."

"But you are not a Wandsman."

"No."

"What are you?"

Stark shrugged. "A man from another world. Or if you wish, a demon, as the little Ochar said. In any case, no enemy to the Hann. Will you make truce according to your custom and listen to what I have to say?"

"Suppose I do that," said the chief, "and my people do not like what they hear."

"Then I shall bid them good-bye and go in peace."

"You swear this?"

"By what? The word of a demon? I have said what I will do."

The chief looked again at the hounds.

"Have I a choice in the matter?"

Stark said, "No."

"Then I will make truce and the Hann shall hear you. But the hounds must not kill."

"They will not unless weapons are drawn against us."

"None shall be drawn." The chief held out his right hand. "I am Ildann, Hearth-Keeper of the Hann."

"I am Stark." He clasped the chief's wiry wrist, felt his clasped in return and knew that Ildann was testing his flesh to see what it was made of.

"From another world?" said Ildann scornfully. "Many tales have come up from the south and down

57

across the mountains, but they're no more than tales told round a winter fire. You're flesh and blood and hard bone like myself—no demon, and not a man either by our standards, but only meat from some Southron sty."

Stark's fingers tightened on the man's wrist. He said softly, "Yet I lead the Northhounds."

Ildann looked into Stark's eyes. He looked away. "I will not forget that."

Stark released his grip. "We will go to your village."

The two groups joined uneasily together, side by side but not mingling. And Jofr said incredulously, "Are you not going to kill them?"

"Not immediately," said Ildann, watching the hounds. Gerd gave him one baleful glance and a warning growl.

The village was in a wide valley, with a glimpse of mountains farther on beyond its rim of hills; not great mountains like the barrier range, but a curiously gnawed-looking line of peaks. In old times there had been a river here. Now it was dry except at the spring flooding, but there was still water in deep tanks dug in the riverbed. Beasts walked patiently around great creaking wheels, and women were busy with the preparation of the soil for the spring sowing. Herds of beasts cropped at some dark scanty herbage that looked more like lichen than grass; perhaps it was something in between, and Stark wondered what sort of crops grew in this place.

The women and the beasts alike were guarded by bowmen in little watchtowers set about the fields. And Stark saw the outlines of old cultivation abandoned to the sand and wrecks of old waterwheels beside dry holes.

"Your land draws in," he said.

"It does for all of us," said Ildann, and glanced bitterly at Jofr. "Even for the Ochar. Old Sun grows weaker, no matter how we feed him. Every year the frosts are with us longer, and more water stays locked in the mountain ice, so that there is less for our fields. The summer pastures shrink—"

"And every year the Runners come in greater numbers to eat up your villages."

"What have you, a stranger, to do with our troubles?" Ildann's gaze was fiercely proud, and the word he used for "stranger" bore connotations of deadly insult. Stark chose to ignore them.

"Is it not the same for all the Lesser Hearths of Kheb?"

Ildann did not answer, and Jofr said impudently, "The Green Cloaks are almost wiped out, the Brown and the Yellow are—"

The man whose saddle he was sharing slapped him hard across the side of his head. Jofr's face screwed up with pain. He said, "I am an Ochar, and my father is a chief."

"Neither statement is a recommendation," said the man, and cuffed him again. "Among the Hann little whelps are silent unless they are told to speak."

Jofr bit his lips. His eyes were full of hate, some for the Hann, most of it for Stark.

The village was protected by a wall that had watchtowers set at irregular intervals. The beehive houses, little more than domed roofs over cellars dug deep in the ground for warmth and protection against the wind, were painted in gay designs, all worn and faded. Narrow lanes dodged and twisted among the domes, and in the center of the village was an open space, roughly circular, with a clump of gnarled, dusty, leather-leaved trees growing in the middle of it.

In the grove was the mud-brick house that held the Hearth and the sacred fire of the tribe of Hann.

Ildann led the way there.

People came out of the houses, away from the wells and wineshops, the market stalls and the washing stones. Even those who had been in the fields came in, until the space around the Hearth-grove was filled with the purple cloaks of the men and the bright-colored skirts of the women. They all watched while Ildann and Stark and the others dismounted and Halk's litter was set carefully on the ground. They watched the grim white hounds, crouching with their eyes half-closed and their jaws half-open. The veiled faces of the men were shadowed beneath their hoods. The faces of the women were closed tight, expressing nothing. They merely watched.

Ildann spoke. A tall woman with proud eyes came out of the Hearth-house, bearing a golden salver on which lay a charred twig. Ildann took up the twig.

"Hearth-right I give you." He marked Stark's forehead with the blackened end of the twig. "If harm befalls you in this place, the same must befall me." He replaced the twig, and the woman went back to tending the Hearth. Ildann spoke to the crowd.

"This man called Stark has come to speak to you. I do not know what he has to say. We will hear him at the second hour after Old Sun's setting."

The crowd made a muttering and rustling. Then it parted as Ildann led his guests away to a house that was set apart from the others. It was larger than most and had two sides to it, one for the chief, the other for guests. The Hooded Men were seminomadic, herdsmen and hunters spending much of the summer on the move after game or pasturage. The bitter winters shut them perforce between walls. The rooms of the guesthouse were small and sparsely furnished, gritty with the everlasting dust but otherwise clean and comfortable enough.

"I'll keep the boy with me," said Ildann. "Don't worry, I'll not waste a fat ransom just to satisfy my spite. Your beasts will be cared for. Everything needful will be brought to you, and I'll send a healer if you wish, to see to your friend there. He looks like a fighting man."

"He is," said Stark, "and I thank you."

The small room had begun to smell strongly of hound, and the minds of the pack were uneasy. They did not like being closed in. Ildann seemed to sense this.

"There is a walled enclosure through that passage, where they can be in the open. No one will disturb them." He watched them as they filed out. "Doubtless

60

you will tell us how it is that these guardians of the Citadel have left their post to follow at your heels."

Stark nodded. "I wish the boy to be there when I speak."

"Whatever you say."

He went out. Halk said, "I wish to be there, too, Dark Man. Now help me out of this damned litter."

They got him onto a bed. Women came and built fires and brought water. One came with herbs and unguents, and Stark watched over her shoulder as she worked. The wound in Halk's side was healing cleanly.

"He needs only rest and food," the woman said, "and time."

Halk looked up at Stark and smiled.

At the second hour after Old Sun's setting, Stark stood under the trees again. Gerd and Grith flanked him to right and left. The remaining seven crouched at his back. Ashton and Gerrith were close by, with Halk in the litter. Ildann stood with the principal men and women of the village, one hand resting firmly on Jofr's shoulder. The Hearth-grove and the open space were lighted by many torches set on poles. The cold dry desert wind shook the flames, sent light snapping and flaring over the folk gathered there, waiting silently, all of them now cloaked and hooded against the chill so that even the faces of the women were hidden.

Ildann said, "We will hear the words of our guest."

His eyes, in the torchlight, were intensely alert. Stark knew that he had spent the last few hours pumping Jofr dry of all the information he possessed. The boy's cockiness had gone; he now appeared angry and doubtful, as if the water had got far too deep for him.

The faceless, voiceless multitude stood patiently. Wind rubbed their leather cloaks together, rattled the tough leaves of the trees. Stark rested his hand on Gerd's head and spoke.

"Your chief has asked me how it is that the North-hounds, the guardians of the Citadel and the Lords Protector, have left their posts to follow me. The answer is plain. There is no longer a Citadel for them to guard. I myself put it to the torch."

61

A wordless cry went round the crowd. Stark let it die away. He turned to Ildann.

"You know this to be true, Hearth-Keeper."

"I know," Ildann said. "The Ochar boy heard, and saw. This man is the Dark Man of the prophecy of Irnan, which has been fulfilled. He and his hounds brought four Wandsmen captive into the wayhouse, and they told Ekmal and his folk that the Lords Protector are fugitives and homeless. There will be no more keeping of the Upper Road by the Ochar, and their lament is very loud."

The cry that came now from the crowd was one of savage pleasure.

Jofr shouted at them furiously. "The Wandsmen have promised us! The Citadel will be rebuilt. My father has sent the Swiftwing, and all the clans of the Ochar will come against you"—he stabbed his finger at Stark—"because of him!"

"That is likely," Stark said. "And I tell you that the Wandsmen would pay a high price for me and for my comrades." He placed his left hand on the head of Grith. "But you would first have to overcome the hounds. Ildann, ask the boy how many Runners were killed by the pack? He saw the bodies."

"I have asked him," Ildann said. "At least half a hundred."

"So you see," Stark said, "that reward would not be easily won. But I can offer you another and greater reward. I offer you freedom from the greed of the Ochar, who want your lands. I offer you freedom from the oppression of the Wandsmen, who support the Ochar. I offer you freedom from the Runners, who eat up your villages. I offer you freedom from hunger and thirst. I offer you Yurunna."

There was a startled silence. Then every tongue began to wag at once.

"Yurunna!" said Ildann fiercely. "You think we have not looked at that place, and often? You think we have not tried? In my father's time, in my grandfather's time . . . The walls are strong. There are many Yur to defend the walls, and they have great machines

62

that scatter fire to burn men where they stand. They have the kennels where the demon hounds are bred, and even the whelps are deadly. How should we take Yurunna?"

"For the Hann alone, or for any of the Lesser Hearths alone, it would not be possible. For all the Lesser Hearths banded together . . ."

Voices rose, shouting about old enmities and blood feuds, raids and killings. The crowd became turbulent. Stark held up his hands.

"If your blood feuds are more important to you than the survival of your tribe, then cling to them! Let the last ember perish from your Hearth, for the sake of them. But why be so foolish? All together, you could be powerful enough to fight the Ochar, to fight anyone except Mother Skaith herself, and you have no choice but to run from her, and that is south. The cold drives the Runners down on you, and you in turn are driven to raid even as far as the Edge. Why should you suffer all this when Yurunna is there for the taking? Would it not be better for Yurunna to feed you, rather than the servants of the Wandsmen?"

There was an uneasy, mumbling quiet while they thought about that.

Ildann voiced the vital question. "Who would lead? No chief of the Lesser Hearths would endure to be made less than any other."

Stark said, "I would lead. I wear no cloak of any color and am at feud with none. I want neither land nor loot, and when my task is done, I leave you." He paused. "It has been foretold that a winged being will blood me among the Hearth-Keepers of Kheb."

Again he waited until the reaction subsided.

"The decision is for you to make. If you decide against me, then I will go and speak to the others. And now I have finished." He turned courteously to Ildann. "What will you have us do?"

"Return to your quarters and wait. We must talk among ourselves."

Back in the guesthouse, they did little talking among themselves. This was the strategy that had been discussed and agreed upon. As fugitives with no resources of their own, they could hope for very little in the way of success, or even survival. With a base of power, even a small one, the odds improved significantly. Yurunna was the bait. Stark had offered it. Now they could only wait and see what the tribesmen would do with it.

"It will go your way," said Gerrith. "Don't worry."

"If it does," said Halk, "well and good. If it doesn't, what has Stark got to worry about? He is no longer the Dark Man, no more fated. He can leave us and run alone back to Skeg. Animal that he is, he might make it. Or again, he might not. No matter. Bring me food and wine. I'm hungry." He lifted his hands and flexed them stiffly. "If we do march south, these must be ready to hold a sword again."

All that night Stark kept waking to hear the sounds of the village, droning and stirring like a disturbed wasp's nest. After Old Sun had been sung up and given wine and fire to begin his day, the summons came from Ildann. Stark went to the house of the chief, and Ashton and Gerrith went with him, as did the two hounds, who would not be left behind.

Ildann had sat all night with his village leaders, both men and women. His eyes were red-rimmed and blinking, but Stark saw in them a glitter of ambition and excitement.

There was something else, too, and its name was fear.

"What do you know of the Fallarin?"

"Nothing," said Stark, "except that the name means 'Chained.' "

"They are the true rulers of this desert. Even the Ochar must bend their stiff necks and pay tribute, as we do."

He brooded. Stark stood patiently.

"They're a blighted race, the Fallarin. In old times the wise men knew how to change people in some sort. They became different—"

"It's called controlled mutation," Stark said. "I've met others. The Children of the Sea-Our-Mother, who live in the water, and the Children of Skaith, who burrow under the Witchfires. Neither meeting was pleasant."

Ildann lifted his shoulders in a peculiar motion of distaste. "The Fallarin wished to be Children of the Sky, but the change was not . . . not as they wanted it. For centuries they have sat in their dark bowl in the mountains, talking to the winds. They are great sorcerers, with power over all the moving air when they wish to use it. We pay them when we sow, when we harvest and when we go to war. All of us. Otherwise they send the sandstorms—"

He looked up sharply. "Is it true, the foretelling of the winged man with the knife?"

"It is true," said Gerrith.

"Well, then," said Ildann, "if the Fallarin will blood you chief, giving you windfavor, the Lesser Hearths will follow wherever you lead."

"Then," said Stark, "I must find the Fallarin."

Ildann nodded. "Tomorrow I go on the spring pilgrimage to the Place of Winds. The Keepers of all the Hearths gather there, under truce. It is forbidden to anyone not of the blood to come there, but I will break custom and take you, if you wish. However, I tell you this."

He leaned forward. "The Fallarin have powers to overcome even your hellhounds, and if they decide against you, you'll end in the flames of the Springfire which is lighted there for Old Sun."

"That may be," said Stark. "Nonetheless, I will go."

"You alone," said Ildann. "The other men have no reason to go, and women are not permitted there. The occasion of the Springfire involves death, and according to our custom women have to do only with the things of life."

Stark did not like the separation, but there seemed no help for it, and Gerrith said:

"All will be well."

Wishing that he could believe that, Stark rode out of the village with Ildann and Jofr and sixty warriors, the Northhounds, a meager string of pack-beasts and two

65

condemned men in cages, to follow the pilgrim standard to the Place of Winds.

II

The pilgrim standard led the way east. A man whose hereditary honor it was rode ahead of the company with the tall staff that bore a pair of outstretched wings. They were wrought in gold with fine workmanship, but they had grown frail with long use, and the wings had been several times broken and clumsily mended. The standard rendered the party safe from attack by members of other tribes. The purple cloaks of the riders drew a streak of somber color across the drab land. They made excellent time. The winds touched them gently. It was always so, Ildann said, when they rode to the gatherings.

Jofr was quiet, glancing frequently at Stark with a certain pointed hopefulness.

Old Sun watched Stark, too, a dull eye full of senile malice. *I'm none of yours,* Stark thought, *and you know it, and you're thinking of the Springfire, like the boy.* He laughed at his own fancy. But the primitive N'Chaka did not laugh. The primitive N'Chaka shivered and was cold, smelling danger on the dim air.

The primitive N'Chaka did not place much faith in visions.

He let the Northhounds run pretty much as they would, keeping Gerd or Grith always by him. Before many miles a pack of Runners appeared. The party was too strong for them to dare an attack. They hung on beyond bowshot, hoping for a straggler or an injured beast. Stark let the eager hounds go at them, and the Hann were impressed. That was the first time the

66

hounds killed along the way. It was not the last. The Runners cared nothing for the pilgrim standard.

Early on the third day a grim wall of mountain rose out of the plain, dark and jagged and alone. It had a look of thunder about it even though the sky was clear, and there was a cleft in the middle of it, like a narrow gate.

At the foot of the cleft, enclosing a kind of bay, a thick stone wall had been erected. Within the wall were the tents and banners of a considerable encampment.

The cavalcade halted, straightened lines, shook dust from cloaks. Purple banners took the wind. A trumpeter set a curved horn to his lips and blew a harsh neighing call of three notes. Stark called the pack to heel. The company moved on toward the wall.

In the wide space between it and the cliff five camps were set up, each one separate with its own staff and its banners, red, brown, green, white and burnt orange for the Ochar. Jofr leaped and cried out; his mount was held tightly so that he could not run.

In the center of the space was a structure of stone slabs perhaps six feet high and twice as broad, with three upright stones set in it, and the whole blackened and stained and cracked from the heat of Old Sun's spring feasting. At least ten cages were dropped haphazardly around the base of the structure, each one holding a man.

Cloaks of the five colors turned out to see the Hann come in. It was a minute or two before they saw Stark and the hounds, and a minute or two more before they believed what they had seen. Then a great cry of anger burst out, and the motley-colored crowd surged forward. The hounds bristled, close around Stark.

Kill, N'Chaka?

Not yet . . .

Ildann held up his arms and shouted. "Wait! It is for the Fallarin to say what shall be done. It has been foretold that they will blood this man a chief . . . Listen to me, you sons of offal! This is the Dark Man

67

of the Southron prophecy, do you hear? The Dark Man! He has brought down the Citadel!"

The crowd stopped its surging and began to listen.

Ildann's voice rang against the cliffs, crying the good news.

"The Citadel has fallen. There'll be no more keeping of the Upper Road—it's dead as a lopped branch above Yurunna, and the Ochar are lopped with it!"

Red, brown, green and white roared with fierce, astonished joy. The roar was followed by a babble of voices. And then, out of a knot of orange cloaks, a tall man spoke.

"You lie."

Ildann thrust Jofr forward. "Tell him, boy. Tell the almighty Romek, Keeper of the Hearth of Ochar."

"It is true, Lord," said Jofr, and bowed his head. "I am Ekmal's son, from the north house—" He stammered out what he knew, and the whold crowd listened. "But the Wandsmen promised, Lord!" he finished. "The Citadel will be rebuilt. And my father has sent the Swiftwing among the clans . . ."

He was drowned out by another roar from the folk of the Lesser Hearths. Stark could see that each of their numbers was less than that of the Ochar. He estimated some hundred and twenty of the orange cloaks, with Ildann's sixty the next largest. All together, the Lesser Hearths did not greatly surpass the Ochar. The Yellow Cloaks were not in yet, but he doubted that they would add more than another twenty or so. These were chief's escorts, the men of honor, but they were probably a fair reflection of the relative numbers of fighting men available to the tribes.

The Ochar closed their ranks, groups of them flowing together out of the press until they formed a solid block of color. They spoke among themselves; and the eyes of Romek, hard cold blue above his facecloth, sought Stark's.

The Lesser Hearths were stirred by currents of motion as men discussed and questioned and thought about the meaning of Ildann's words.

Behind them all was the cleft. Shadows clotted thick

there. Stark could not see into it. The wind made strange sounds passing through. Stark could imagine that it talked a secret language of its own, telling all that happened below. And if the wind talked, surely someone listened.

Romek stepped forward. He questioned Jofr, making him tell again the story of how Stark and the hounds came to the wayhouse. Then he said:

"It seems certain that this outlander has done a great wrong. Since it touches us, it is for us to deal with him."

"And take him back to the Wandsmen, no doubt," said Ildann, "to make your masters happy."

"He is nothing to you," said Romek. "Stand aside."

"You're forgetting the Northhounds," said Ildann. "Surely you know them? But try if you like."

Romek hesitated. Nine pairs of baleful eyes regarded him. Ildann shouted again to the red cloaks and the white, the brown and the green.

"The Dark Man has brought down the Citadel. Now he will bring down Yurunna."

"Yurunna!" they cried. "How? How?"

"If we will join our forces together, he will lead us. If the Fallarin blood him. Only if the Fallarin blood him! He is not of our race, and his feud is only with the Wandsmen. Because of that feud he offers us Yurunna. Yurunna! Food, water, safety from the Runners. Life! Yurunna!"

It sounded like a battle cry.

When he could make himself heard, Romek said, "That would mean war with the Ochar. We would sweep the desert clean."

"Perhaps not!" shouted the chief of the Brown Cloaks. "And if we should take Yurunna, the First-Come would be the Last!"

Hate was in the laughter that followed. Old and bitter hate. Romek heard it. He took it as a thing of pride. He looked at the Northhounds, and he looked at Stark, and he nodded his cowled head.

"All this will happen only if the Fallarin blood him. Very well. Let him go to the Fallarin and ask them for windfavor. And when they've heard him out, we shall see where he goes—to Yurunna, or to the Spring-fire."

"He will go to the Fallarin when he is bidden," said Ildann.

"No," said Stark. "I will go now."

"But you cannot," said Ildann, all bravery gone from his voice. "No one enters there without permission."

"I will," said Stark.

He rode forward with the hounds beside him. The sound in their throats was like muted thunder, and the Hooded Men stood back to let them pass. Stark did not look back to see whether Ildann came with him. He moved without haste past the place of the Spring-fire and the cages where the victims waited, stripped of cloaks and wrappings so that he could see their despairing faces white as snow except for a ludicrous band of brown across the eyes.

He moved toward the cleft, the narrow gateway in the cliff.

Ildann did not follow him into that windy darkness.

The way was only wide enough for a single rider, and very steep. The soft furred paws of the beast and the pads of the hounds made only the smallest scuffling on bare rock. It was cold there, with the tomb-chill of sunless places, and the wind talked. Stark thought that he could understand the words.

Sometimes the wind laughed, and the laughter was not friendly.

Things, said Gerd.

I know. There were galleries high up under the ragged streak of sky. He was aware of movement there, crouchings and scuttlings. He knew, although he could not see them, that there were piles of boulders ready to be sent crashing on his head.

Watch.

N'Chaka! Cannot watch. Minds not speak. Cannot hear!

And the wind talked.

The cleft ended at a wall of rock that had a single opening through which one man might pass.

Stark left the beast. Beyond the opening was a stair that spiraled sharply upward into darkness.

Stark climbed, the hounds behind him, alarmed, muttering, their breathing loud in the closed space. At length he saw the top of the stair and a tall thin doorway with light on the other side.

A creature sat in the doorway looking down at him from under slitted eyelids.

12

It was hairless and horny; and it had four arms that appeared to be very limber and strong, without joints, each arm ending in three tentacular fingers. It opened a beaky mouth and said:

"I am Klatlekt. I keep the door. Who comes to the Place of Winds?"

"I am Stark," he said. "A stranger. I seek audience with the Fallarin."

"You have not been bidden."

"I am here."

The blinking green-gold gaze shifted to the hounds. "You have with you four-footed things whose minds are black and burning."

N'Chaka! It does not fear. Mind not touch.

"They will do no harm," Stark said, "unless harm is done."

"They can do no harm," said Klatlekt. "They are harmless."

N'Chaka. Strange . . .

The hounds whimpered. Stark mounted one more step.

"Never mind the hounds. Your masters wish to see me. Otherwise we would not have reached this door."

"For good or ill," said the doorkeeper. "Come, then."

It rose and led the way. Stark followed, through the tall thin door. The hounds padded after, reluctant.

Cannot touch, N'Chaka. Cannot touch.

They stood in a great bowl surrounded by cliffs of somber rock that shaded from gray to slaty black. The cliffs were high, so that Old Sun never saw the bottom of the bowl, which was carpeted with a moss that felt gravelly rather than soft underfoot.

All around the bowl the rock of the cliffs had been cut and carved into free-standing forms that pulled the gaze upward to the sky, so that Stark felt giddy, as if he might fall that way. It seemed that all the winds of the desert and the currents of the high air had been caught as they passed by and frozen here into stony rising thermals and purling waves and circling whirlwinds that seemed in that twilight to spring and flow. But they did not. They were firmly anchored, and the true air was utterly still. There was no sign of living things except for Stark and the hounds and the one called Klatlekt.

Yet there were living things, and Stark knew it, and so did the hounds.

Things. Watch.

The rock behind the carved wind patterns was honeycombed with secret openings. The hounds growled and shivered, pressing close. They were fearful now for the first time in their lives, their power of death useless against nonhuman minds.

Klatlekt pointed three slender fingers to a raised round platform of stone blocks in the center of the bowl. At the king-point of the circle stood a great carved seat shaped like a wind-devil.

"Go there."

Stark mounted broad steps, the hounds slinking at heel.

Minds up there can touch. Kill?

No!

Klatlekt had disappeared. Stark stood. He listened to the silence that was not quite silent, and the hairs rose at the back of his neck.

A little wind came. It fingered his hair. It went

72

snuffling lightly down the height of him and across the breadth of him, and then it flickered cold across his face, and he thought that some of it went in at his eyes and blew swiftly through the windings of his brain. It pulled free of him with a tiny chuckle and went to pluck at the hounds and set them whimpering with their fur all awry.

N'Chaka!

Still. Still.

It was not easy to be still.

The small wind went away.

Stark waited, listening to sounds he could not quite hear.

All at once there was sound and enough; the rushing susurration of half a thousand pairs of wings a-beat on the air. The Fallarin flitted from their doorways, to stand among their rising thermals and graceful whirl-winds.

Stark continued to wait.

One came alone, from between two curling ribbons of stone that overarched the largest opening. He wore a brief kilt of scarlet leather. A golden girdle clasped his waist, and a king's torque circled his neck. Otherwise he was clad in close dark fur against the cold. His body was small and spare and light. The wings that sprang from his shoulders were dark-leathered and strong, and when he descended to the platform his movement was assured, if not beautiful. But Stark knew why they were called the Chained. The genetic alteration their ancestors had undergone, hoping to give their descendants new life on a dying world, had cheated them cruelly. That inadequate wingspan would never know the freedom of the high air.

"Yes," said the Fallarin, "we are clipped birds, a mockery above and below." He stood before the high seat, looking straight up into Stark's eyes; his own were yellow as a falcon's, but too full of a dark wisdom for even that royal bird. His face was narrow and harsh, too strong for beauty, with a sharp nose and jutting chin. But when he smiled he was handsome, as a sword is handsome.

"I am Alderyk, and king in this place."

Round the circumference of the bowl, from lower galleries, a considerable number of the four-armed things had appeared. They stood quietly, watching. They were not being menacing. They were merely there.

"The Tarf," said Alderyk. "Our excellent servants, created by the same hands that made us, though not of human stock, and with greater care, for they function admirably." His gaze dropped. "You also have your retainers."

The hounds felt the force in him and growled uneasily. Alderyk laughed, a sound not entirely pleasant.

"I know you, hounds. You were made, like us, though you had no choice in that making. You are Skaith-born, like us, and I understand you better than I do your master."

The yellow eyes, somber-bright, returned to Stark.

"You are the future standing there, a strange thing, full of distances I cannot plumb. A black whirling wind to break and scatter, leaving nothing untouched behind you, not even the Fallarin."

His wings spread wide, rustling, then clapped shut. A buffet of air came from nowhere and struck Stark's face like an open palm.

"I do not altogether like you."

"Liking is neither here nor there," said Stark mildly. "You seem to know me."

"We know you, Stark. We live solitary here in our eyrie, but the winds bring us news from all the world."

And perhaps they do, thought Stark. And there are also the Harsenyi and the Ochar to peddle whatever tales go up and down the roads of Skaith. The whole north had known about Ashton being brought to the Citadel, a man from another world, and the prophecy of Irnan had followed hard on his heels. The Wandsmen themselves had spread knowledge of Stark throughout the darklands in their eagerness to capture him. It would have been strange if the Fallarin did not know all about the events that were beginning to shake the foundations of their world.

"We knew of the prophecy," said Alderyk. "It was interesting to speculate on the possibility of its fulfillment."

"If the winds bring you news from as far away as Skeg and the city-states, surely there's a breeze that whispers from your own doorstep."

"We heard all that was said there. And perhaps . . ." He cocked his dark head birdwise and smiled. "Perhaps we heard you speak by the Hearth of Hann. Perhaps, even, we heard the sun-haired woman talk of blooding in a place of rocks."

That startled Stark, though not greatly. The Fallarin had the power to move winds—sorcery or psychokinetics, the name mattered little—and it was not unlikely that they could see and hear farther than most, even if it was simply a matter of reading his mind.

"Then you know why Ildann brought me here. You know what I want from you. Tell me what you want from me."

Alderyk ceased smiling. "That," he said, "we have not yet decided." He turned and signaled to one of the Tarf. It scuttled quickly into a doorway, and up on their high perches the Fallarin clapped their thousand wings, and an angry gale whirled snarling around the cliffs. The hounds whined dismally.

The Tarf came back, bearing something on one of its arms. It climbed to the platform and came to Alderyk, who said:

"Let him see the thing clearly."

The thing was a huge proud bird, feathered all in bronze and iron. It fretted because its feet were bound and its head hooded with a bit of cloth. Ever and again it opened its beak and cried out harshly, and Stark understood the word it spoke.

"It is a Swiftwing," he said, remembering the bronze-and-iron flash in the sky, "and it calls for war. It belongs to a chief named Ekmal."

"I think it is his son you have out there."

"I was told that he would be my guide to this place. No harm has come to him."

"Nonetheless, Ekmal calls the clans to war."

75

Stark shook his head. "The Wandsmen call for war because of the Citadel. They are determined to have me prisoner, or dead, along with my friends. The boy is safe enough, and Ekmal knows it."

"A fine witches' brew you've set boiling in our northland," Alderyk said. The Fallarin hissed, and again the wind surged angrily. "The Swiftwing came to seek out Romek, the Ochar Hearth-Keeper. We brought it here instead. The creatures are winged powerfully, but they cannot fly against our currents. We wished to know more before we let Romek have its summons."

He motioned the Tarf away. It withdrew to the east point of the platform, gentling the great bird. Alderyk's eyes held Stark's, yellow and cruel.

"You ask for windfavor as war chief of all the Lesser Hearths, to take Yurunna from the Wandsmen. Why should we grant it, when it means war with all the Ochar? Why should we not give you to Romek for the Wandsmen, or to the Springfire to feed Old Sun?"

Stark said, "Old Sun will grow no stronger no matter how you feed him. He is dying, and the north closes in. This is true for you as it is for the Lesser Hearths, and for the Ochar, too, though they don't accept it—they think the Wandsmen can keep them fed forever."

"And can they not?"

"The Wandsmen will decide that, not the Ochar. There is revolt in the south. Things have changed with the coming of the ships to Skeg. Too many folk hate the Wandsmen and wish to find better worlds to live in. There may be a breaking of power."

"Will be," said Alderyk, "if you have your way. Why should we let you use the Lesser Hearths to gain your own ends?"

"You live on the tribute from these people. Surely you know better than I how scant it grows."

There was a rustling of wings and a sigh from the high perches. Alderyk's eyes were two points of yellow fire, burning into Stark's mind.

"Are you saying that we too must leave our place

76

where we have lived for centuries and find ourselves a better world?"

Wind buffeted Stark from all sides, deafened him, caught the breath from his mouth. The hounds cowered. When the wind died away he said, "The north-folk must move sooner or later for their lives. The Lesser Hearths are dying out. The Wandsmen are interested only in retaining their power, and where they must sacrifice to do so, they will. Make your own choice, but you would be wise to leave a road south open for yourselves when you choose to take it. In the meantime there is enough at Yurunna for all, if you control it."

Silence. The stillness of dead air.

"And you would lead?"

"Yes."

There was a sudden commotion among the Tarf, and one of them came rushing across the open and onto the platform, to crouch at Alderyk's feet.

"Lord," it said, clicking and rattling in its shocked haste, "there has been a killing below. The pilgrim truce is broken, and the Ochar hold the entrance to the cleft."

13

For one long moment Alderyk neither moved nor looked away from Stark.

"A black wind, to break and scatter . . ."

Up along the high perches the ranks of the Fallarin moved and shifted, with a hissing of wings and voices. Stark braced himself for an assault. None came. Yet the air was so charged that he looked for lightning bolts to play between the twilit cliffs.

As though he had come to some decision, Alderyk turned abruptly to the Tarf.

"Bid Romek come to me with no more than six of his men of honor. And say that if the peace is not kept, I will send such wrath upon them as they have never seen."

The Tarf went away.

Stark wondered what had happened below, and how many were dead, and whether Ildann was among them.

"Stand back," said Alderyk. "There. And keep your hellhounds quiet."

He sat himself on the high seat that was like a wind devil, and there was thunder on his brow.

Stark went where he was told, to the west point of the circle, opposite the place where the Tarf still gentled the Swiftwing. The hounds were unhappy, sensing great forces about them that they could neither understand nor fight. It was all Stark could do to hold them. His own muscles were tight with strain, and the sweat ran on him. He was acutely aware of the high cliffs and the one narrow door. If things went against him, it was not going to be easy to fight his way out.

He hated the Tarf with their round unhuman heads and their unhuman brains that cared not a fig for Northhounds.

The Ochar, at least, were no more than human.

They entered the bowl, bright orange cloaks dulled in that sunless gloom. They walked across the mossy open ground and mounted the steps to the platform.

Romek saw the Swiftwing and checked. Then he spoke angrily to Alderyk.

"Why have you held this summons from me?"

"Because I wished to," Alderyk said, "and why have you broken truce?"

"Ildann stirred up mischief among the Lesser Hearths. There were high words, and then blows, and some hot head drew a knife. My man only defended himself."

It crossed Stark's mind that if the Fallarin knew all that happened on their doorstep, Alderyk must have known this, too. Had he been unable to prevent it? Or had he let it happen?

"How many are dead?"

"One only." Romek's shoulders lifted slightly. "A Brown Cloak."

"One or a hundred, it's death and forbidden." Alderyk's head went sidewise, in the way Stark was beginning to know. "What are your men defending now?"

A wind, very soft and tigerish, prowled the cliffs.

"The peace," said Romek, and looked at Stark.

"Ah," said Alderyk. "You think there might be trouble if Stark is brought to the Springfire."

In a cold flat unflinching voice Romek said, "There will be worse trouble if he is not. You see the Swiftwing. All the clans of the Ochar are rousing for war, and this man is the cause. If he dies now in the Springfire, with the Keepers of the Lesser Hearths there to see it, then the threat will end."

"But suppose," said Alderyk, "just suppose that we have decided to give him windfavor?"

"You would not be so foolish," Romek said.

"Wise Romek. Tell me why."

"Because it is on the tribute of the Ochar, more than all the others, that you stay alive—and that tribute comes from the Wandsmen more than it does from us." The orange cloth hid Romek's face, but even so it was plain that a smile was on his mouth and that the smile was insolent. "No matter how the winds blow, the Ochar will be fed."

"I see," said Alderyk. "And we will not?"

Romek's hand made a sweeping gesture. "I didn't say that."

"True, you didn't say it."

"There can be no such talk between allies. Give us the man, Alderyk, and we'll see that the peace is kept."

Stark held tight to Gerd's bristling neck on the one side and Grith's on the other.

Wait. Wait . . .

Alderyk stood up. In spite of his smallness he

seemed to overtop the towering Ochar. He spoke to his people, calmly and without passion.

"You have heard all that has passed here. We are given a choice, between peace and war, between starvation and the bounty of the Ochar. How do you choose, then? Which shall I give to Romek—Stark or the Swiftwing?"

Dark wings clattered. Winds whirled around the cliffs, reached out to catch at Romek's cloak and hood and tear away his veil so that he stood naked-faced, white and shamed before them all.

"Give him the Swiftwing!"

Alderyk motioned to the Tarf, which moved forward and held out its arm.

Romek took the Swiftwing. With steady fingers he undid the thong that held the bird's feet and loosed the wrapping from its head. It opened eyes like two red stars and looked at him and cried out, "War!"

"Yes," said Romek softly. "War."

He flung the bird upward. It took the air, beating powerfully, circling higher and higher until it gained the sunlight and was gone.

Alderyk said, "From this day the Place of Winds is barred to the Ochar. Now go."

Romek turned and stalked out with his men.

"Come here," Alderyk said to Stark, and sat again upon the high seat, his face hard and grim. "We too have watched the north close in. We have had our eyes on Yurunna and the growing insolence of the Ochar. We lacked two things, strength and a leader. You offer us both. So we gamble, because if we do not we shall become the cut dogs of the Wandsmen even as the Ochar have." His yellow gaze struck deep into Stark, and a shiver of air ran whirling up the stony curves of the seat. "We gamble, Stark. Let us hope we don't lose."

They waited until the yellow Qard came in, just before sundown. That night, while torches flared and light spilled from all the high doorways of the Fallarin, Stark was blooded war chief of the Lesser Hearths of Kheb, mingling his blood with the blood of

80

the Hearth-Keepers, beginning with Ildann, and sprinkling a little more on the stones for Old Sun. Alderyk held the knife. When all else was done, he made a slash in the dark fur of his own wrist and marked Stark's forehead with a purling line.

"I give you windfavor. May you use it well."

Off to one side, where he had been brought for safekeeping, Jofr crouched and hugged his knees and wept with rage and hate.

A little more than three weeks later, duly ransomed, he sat beside his father on the crest of a long dune and saw what made him forget his tears.

Splashed across the dun landscape below, in patches of faded color, was an army, mounted, glittering with spears. The patches of color were purple and red and brown. One-half of the six Lesser Hearths.

Spread out along the dune, a great mass of burnt orange, was the army of the Ochar. Even the inexperienced eyes of a boy on his first warfaring could see that the extent of the orange line was double that of the purple and red and brown together.

Jofr laughed and drummed his heels on the flanks of his mount.

Farther away on that height Gelmar of Skeg looked down and spoke to Romek.

"Good. The First-Come have done well." He was robed and hooded like an Ochar, having no wish to draw attention to himself.

"We could always move more quickly than that rabble," said Romek, and added contemptuously, "So far, the Fallarin have done nothing to hinder us. Perhaps they have been remembering where their interests lie." He sought out the distant purple banner that marked Ildann's place in the line of battle that was being formed out of the interrupted march. "The man Stark will be there, most likely."

But Stark was nowhere in that army.

14

Stark was herding Runners.

After he was blooded, he had let the Hooded Men do what they would at the ceremony of the Spring-fire, taking no part in it himself. The Ochar had left in a tremendous hurry. Romek would be setting about organizing his army as swiftly as possible. Stark had talked strategy with the Fallarin. During those talks he had come to the conclusion that the Fallarin had acquired, down through the centuries, a streak of mad-ness.

He had sent the Hearth-Keepers away from the Place of Winds to gather their men as quickly as they might, knowing even then that the Ochar, who had be-gun mustering days before and were less widely scat-tered, would be ready in force sooner than they could be no matter how they ran. Purple Hann, brown Marag and red Kref could gather most quickly. The other three Hearths were more distant.

By common consent a rendezvous was chosen, a place called the Tears of Lek, a salt lake not far above Yurunna.

But it was certain, unless the Ochar had lost all their skill and Gelmar of Skeg all his cunning, that the army of the Lesser Hearths would not be permitted to join its several parts together at its leisure.

Ildann said, "We three—Hann, Marag and Kref—being the nearest, will surely bear the brunt. We're strong fighters and not afraid to die, but no amount of courage will stand off the Ochar for long."

Alderyk smiled his sharp cruel smile, and the wings of the Fallarin beat up a laughing howl of wind.

"We'll see to it that you have help."

· And Stark had stroked Gerd's ugly head and nodded, hoping that he was not lying. Because if he was, the fierce-eyed chiefs would be leading their people to certain death, in his name.

So now, like a careful shepherd, Stark moved across the dunes on the broad track of the Ochar host; and the Northhounds ran free, bounding at the edges of the stinking, tattered and thoroughly cowed flock, flicking them with the lash of terror.

They had gathered up between three and four hundred of the things, cleaning out three nesting cities with fire and wind and hound-fear. Beside Stark and the pack, one hundred and fifty Fallarin—with Alderyk at their head and twice as many Tarf to serve them—managed the Runners with small bursts of sandstorm, guiding them and holding down their speed.

The Fallarin rode, like Stark. When they did take the air, their flight was short and skimming. The Tarf went on their own limbs, and they could outrun anything except the Runners. Stark had used them as scouts, depending on their information for the timing of this unlikely operation. He had considered the whole idea insane, but the Fallarin had been serenely confident, knowing their own skills and the habits of Runners.

"Runner packs always go *with* the sandstorms, and just ahead," Alderyk said. "They never go against them. We can drive them wherever we wish them to go, using the wind for a whip."

And so far they had done just that. Whenever the Runners tried to turn or scatter, they were met by a rush of stinging sand, and they turned again to go before it.

Now Alderyk rode up beside Stark and said, "Look at them. They smell meat."

The runners had begun to move faster. They were forgetting the hounds. Some of the old males made hooting cries.

"Suppose it's our own people they hit," Stark said. The Tarf had kept him in close touch with the movements of both armies, and he knew that Ildann's force was facing the Ochar.

"They won't," said Alderyk. "Be ready about your hounds, and keep out of our way."

Two Tarf came racing back, kicking spurts of sand. "Beyond that next rise, Lord, we could see a great patch of orange moving."

Alderyk said, "I will go myself."

One of the Tarf caught his bridle. He launched himself with a leathery flapping and rose heavily into the air; not high, but high enough to see farther than anyone on the ground.

He went a little distance forward and then came back in a great hurry.

"Now!" he said to Stark. "Ildann's army lies there, to your left, across two ridges." He cried out a shrill cry to the Fallarin.

Stark called in his hounds.

War-horns sounded out of sight beyond the dunes, hoarse and bawling.

The Fallarin were ranged in a wide crescent whose points enclosed the Runners. Stark rode through their line, out of the way of it. He saw them spread their wings. He heard them begin to sing, a strange wild crooning storm-song, and underneath the singing the wings beat a broken cadence.

The hounds howled.

Within the crescent the wind rose shrieking and the sand rose with it in a blinding wall. The blurred mass of the Runners moved, picking up speed, all the narrow bodies thrust forward, the incredible legs churning.

The sand hid them. Wind and cloud rushed away. Stark put his beast into a loping run, the hounds beside him.

He cleared the first dune, plunged in the hollow beyond it, going at a tangent behind that flying wall of sand. He began to hear noises, horns blowing, a confusion of shouts and cries almost lost in the wind-roar. When he reached the crest of the second dune, he could see what was happening.

Ildann had drawn his line on a wide flat. The Ochar had launched their attack from the height, throwing out wings on eitiher side to take advantage of their greater numbers and envelop the smaller army.

The sandstorm of the Fallarin, with its several hundred Runners, hit the Ochar left wing before it was halfway down the slope of the dune.

The shock was audible. The mass of burnt orange disintegrated in a boiling of sand and leaping bodies. Hideous sounds came out of that turmoil, where the Runners tore, and fed, and died.

War-horns bellowed. Men shouted. The sounds were thin and lost. The charge faltered as the line staggered, struggled to reform itself.

Momentum carried right and center down the slope. Arrows flew from both sides. Ildann's line wheeled, raggedly but with savage enthusiasm, purple and brown taking the burnt of the shock while the red Kref spurred up to drive a wedge between the Ochar center and the totally demoralized left.

They struck hard. But Stark's heart sank when he saw the solid wall of orange that still confronted them.

He kicked the beast into a run, going down the slope toward the battle.

The sand was settling. Knots of men and beasts and Runners heaved and floundered, inextricably mixed, among the dead and dying. Suddenly at the Ochar rear a whirlwind rose and struck, spouting up more sand. Torn scraps of orange flew out of it like winter leaves. The Fallarin had moved on to fresh endeavors. The Ochar line swayed and shifted, and the men of the Lesser Hearths howled like wolves.

With his spear leveled and the hounds death-baying around him, Stark went into the fight.

He went bareheaded and barefaced, and that alone marked him. The Red Cloaks cheered and shouted his name. The hounds killed a way for him through the orange, toward where Romek's standard showed above the melee, opposite Ildann's center.

Many of the men on both sides fought on foot now. The ground was littered with dead beasts and the dusty cloaks of the fallen. Over the roar of battle came the sound of the whirling winds, dancing their devil's dance, stripping men of their garments, beating and blinding them, tossing them like chaff, driving their mounts mad with fear.

The Ochar flinched and reeled. Battered from all sides, they began to break and scatter, and the whirlwinds drove them. The men of the Lesser Hearths pressed furiously against the yielding line.

Romek's standard still stood. He had his clansmen by him, a hundred or more still unwounded. He saw Stark, at the head of the Purple Cloaks and coming strongly. Romek raised his standard and shouted. His men charged Ildann's center.

Romek came straight for Stark.

Let be, said Stark to the hounds. *Guard yourselves.*

He spurred forward to meet the Keeper of the Hearth of Ochar.

The first spear clash snapped shafts against small round shields and toppled both men unhurt from the saddle. Drawing blade, they fought on foot, with the tides of purple and orange flowing round them on all sides and a banshee screaming of wind beyond. Romek was a tall cold fury quite careless of life if he could only take Stark with him.

Kill? said Gerd, clawing the ground. *Kill, N'Chaka? No. This one must be mine.*

There were plenty of others. The hounds killed themselves weary.

Gradually Stark became aware of a small quietness in which he and Romek circled and slashed and parried. There was only the stamp of their feet and the ringing blades and a huge sound of breathing. They were surrounded by purple cloaks.

Romek, steel and rawhide, cut and slashed until his arm began to tire. Stark moved like a wraith. The level light of Old Sun caught in his pale eyes, and there was a patience there as terrible as time.

Romek's soft boots shuffled in the trodden sand. Shuffled, missed step. Stumbled.

Stark leaped forward.

86

Romek struck, low and viciously, out of that feint.

Stark leaned aside, as an animal shifts weight in mid-spring. The blade sang past him. His arm whipped down. The curved edge of his blade took Romek between shoulder and jaw.

Gerd came and sniffed at the severed head. Then he licked Stark's hand.

Ildann, his cloak torn and bloody, shook his sword in the air.

"Where are the Ochar? Where is the pride of the First-Come?"

A great wild shout went up. The men would have taken Stark on their shoulders; something held them back, and it was not entirely the presence of the hounds.

Stark thrust his blade into the sand to clean it. The battle was over, except for the noisy business of stamping down the last bits of it and slaughtering those Runners that were still alive and too stupid to escape. The whirlwinds danced over the dunes, flogging the surviving Ochar on their way.

Stark said to Ildann, "Where are my companions?"

"Yonder behind the ridge, there." He pointed across the flat. "We left them with the baggage train and a strong guard. They'll be coming soon."

"Did you see . . . Was there a stranger with Romek at any time?"

"A Wandsman? No, I saw none."

"Pass the word along. If a stranger is found among the dead, I want to know it."

Ildann passed the word. But Gelmar was not among the dead. He was fighting hard to stay among the living, clinging to his racing beast and thinking of Yurunna and the Lords Protector.

Jofr was not among the dead, either. Some of the Hann found him half-dazed where the wind had flung him, and they brought him to headquarters instead of slitting his throat because they remembered the ransom.

Stark was there with Gerrith and Ashton and Halk, and the three Hearth-Keepers, and Alderyk of the Fallarin. He looked at the boy, all beaten and drooping between the tall men.

"Let him sit," he said. There was a tiny fire and the air was chill. "Bring him food and water."

Jofr kept his head bent down and would not touch what was brought to him. Ashton sat by and watched him.

Stark asked Gerrith, "Do we have any further need of this one?"

"No."

Stark turned to Alderyk. "Perhaps some of your Tarf could take him where he can find his own people."

"That would be easy enough. But why do you want to save him?"

"He's only a child."

"Very well, if you must. They can start now."

The three chiefs began to talk about ransom.

Stark said to the boy, "Is your father living?"

"I don't know. I lost him when the wind struck."

"You see?" said Stark to the chiefs. "And even if Ekmal did survive, he will have little to spare for ransoms. Think of the loot of Yurunna. Get up, boy."

Jofr sighed and made as though to rise. Instead, he flung himself across the fire, straight at Stark's throat, and there was in his hand a small knife with which he was used to cut meat.

Stark caught his hand and Ashton his feet. The knife dropped.

"That's why he refused your bread and salt," said Ashton. "I told you it was a blue-eyed viper."

Stark smiled. "It's a brave one, at any rate." He shook the boy and set him on his feet. "Get home to your mother."

Jofr went away with his guards, and he was weeping again, this time with sheer frustration. The blade had come so close.

Hann, Kref and Marag slaughtered the too sorely wounded with due honor and ceremony and buried their dead. Runners came out of nowhere to dispose of the Ochar.

88

The army gathered itself and moved on, traveling swiftly toward the bitter lake.

The Tears of Lek shone sullenly under Old Sun like an unpolished shield dropped in the midst of desolation. Its heavy waters never froze even in the dead of winter. White salt pans gleamed, scarred by generations of quarrying. On the unfriendly surround of stiff sedges and sand, the camps of green Thorn and white Thuran were set up. The yellow Qard as usual, were late.

Camp was made, and the men began celebrating their victory. Thorn and Thuran were as savagely joyful as the actual victors. They sang harsh yelping songs and did leaping dances to the rattle of small drums and the shrilling of pipes. This went on all night, and there was almost a second war when it seemed to Hann, Marag and Kref that their newly made and so far non-fighting brothers were taking too large a part in the rejoicing.

In the red morning Stark and Ashton, with Alderyk and the chiefs, rode out to a line of untidy hills and climbed to a place where they could overlook Yurunna.

From this distance it was not the city that took the eye so much as the oasis that surrounded it.

There was water, in plenty. Sunlight glinted on irrigation ditches, a spidery pattern amid the fields. Things were a lot further along here than at Ildann's village. Color smeared the land in patches; sickly yellow, greenish black, dusty ocher, leprous white. There were orchards of spiny twisted trees. To Stark, it was supremely unlovely. To the tribesmen, it was paradise.

In the midst of this ugly garden, some careless titan had dropped a huge grim rock, and on top of the rock someone had built a darkness. There was little detail to be seen this far away, but that was the impression Stark had, a walled and brooding darkness above the gloomy fields.

"You see how it stands, Eric," Ashton said. "Not pretty, but rich and fat all the same. And alone. Every

89

hungry tribesman who ever passed this way has looked at it and plotted how to take it."

"And sometimes tried," said Ildann. "Oh, yes. tried."

"The Wandsmen keep the city well prepared. A caravan came in while I was there, bringing military stores, oil and the stuff they call *kheffi*, some kind of resinous fiber that makes the spreading fire when it's soaked and lighted. There were timbers and cordage to repair the ballistas, and there were weapons. They train the Yur well and keep them trained, about a thousand of them. Yurunna is vital to their presence here in the north, and they know that even the best-bought loyalty, such as they have from the Ochar, ought not to be tempted with weakness."

"Very formidable," said Alderyk.

"Yes."

"Impregnable?"

"Certainly difficult."

"For ordinary humans, yes," said Alderyk.

He clapped his wings and cried a vaulting cry. Dust whipped across the desert, and a long while later Stark saw trees in the oasis bend to a sudden gust.

The yellow Qard came in that afternoon. The next day the army marched and set down before Yurunna.

15

High on its rock, the city scragged the sky like the top of a shattered tree stump. A wall encircled it, high and tight. Buildings stretched up to peer over with narrow eyes. Steep roofs gave back a hard gleaming in the rusty light of Old Sun, except where there were empty gaps.

A single road, wide enough for a cart, zigzagged

up the western face of the rock to the single gate. The gate, Ashton said, was fashioned of black iron and very strong. It was set deep between two flanking towers. On the tops of these towers great cauldrons were set, with engines for casting the spreading fire.

At other places around the wall other engines were set. Yur in polished leather manned the wall, and now and again a Wandsman passed along it with a couple of hounds in leash. The wall was sheer and smooth, thirty feet or so atop seventy or eighty of sheer cliff.

Lacking modern weapons, lacking even primitive siege engines, the invaders faced a city that seemed impregnable.

But that night the attack on Yurunna began, though not one man of the Lesser Hearths dight himself for war.

The men drummed and danced and piped and sang or did otherwise as it pleased them. But there was another singing, and that came from the camp of the Fallarin, where the Tarf stood guard in a silent circle, armed with four-handed swords.

The singing was sprightly and wicked and mischievous and cruel, and under it like a whispering base was the sound of wings a-beat.

Up in the city a small wind began to prowl.

It skipped on roof tiles and ran along narrow streets. It poked and whined into holes and corners. It climbed old walls and felt the texture and the weakness of them. It puffed at cressets, torches, lamps. It snuffed wood.

It grew.

It became a hundred winds.

Yurunna was old, a palimpsest, city built upon half-obliterated city as this people and that came down from the north and took it and held it and then left it again for the next wave of wanderers. Some of the buildings were stout, solid stone. Some were built in part of timber brought up from the south, using one or two walls of an older shell so that the wooden structures resembled the nests of mud-dauber wasps plastered to the stone. In the center of the city and in the

91

area around the gate the buildings were used and lived in. In the small outer quarters of the small city the buildings were unused, except along the wall where the sinews of war were stored ready to hand. These buildings were sound, and kept so. Of the others, some had fallen. Some were ready to fall.

All night long the werewinds laughed and gamed in the narrow ways of Yurunna, and the Yur looked up with their copper-colored eyes like the eyes of dolls and saw deadly roof tiles spin like autumn leaves, shied down at them by the fingers of the wind. Chimneys crumbled. Old walls swayed and shook until they toppled. The dark was full of clatterings and crashings. The Yur women wept in their great house, trembling when the shutters banged open and the curtains blew, scurrying to protect their screaming young.

The Wandsmen, two score of them who oversaw the breeding of Yur and Northhound, the training of the young, the ordering of city and field, were at first scornful of the power of the Fallarin. No wind could threaten their strong walls. They became uneasy as the night wore on and their own city seemed to have been turned against them; had in fact become a weapon in the enemy's hands.

The Northhounds on the wall and in the dark streets shivered, though they had felt far colder winds. They howled dismally, and when walls fell on them they died, and there was no enemy they could strike at. The face of the Houndmaster, already set in the grim lines of a heartstricken man, became more grim.

And that was not the worst.

The werewinds played with fire.

Cressets fell. Torches blew down. Lamps were knocked over. Flames sprang up, and the werewinds blew upon them, fanned them, sucked them up into whirling gold-red storms. The black sky brightened above Yurunna.

The Wandsmen fought the fires with fewer Yur than they would have liked. They dared not strip the wall of defenders for fear of winged men, who might scale the unscalable and let down ropes for the wingless.

Toward dawn, when the fires were to some degree controlled, the werewinds struck in several places, oversetting the cauldrons of oil and the supplies of the spreading fire on the wall, then tossing down the huge basket-torches that burned beside the emplacements. The resultant fires destroyed some of the ballistas, ate their way into some of the nearby storerooms, where there was more oil and more of the *kheffi* for the spreading fire. Wandsmen and Yur had no rest by day.

Stark assumed that the Fallarin rested. He made no attempt to find out. He rode among the tribes, making sure that certain preparations were being carried out.

By evening, the defenders of the city had repaired the damage on the wall, dragging up new ballistas, setting more cauldrons and containers.

When it was full dark, the gay sadistic song began again, with the beating of wings. Again the werewinds prowled and frisked, and destroyed, and killed wherever they could.

Fires were harder to set because this night there were no torches or cressets or lamps in the city. They managed even so. They puffed old embers to life and tumbled more cauldrons and torches, throwing ballistas and crews from the wall and from the towers by the gate. At dawn there was a pall of smoke over Yurunna, and no rest within it.

For three long nights the werewinds made Yurunna their playground. On the morning of the fourth day Alderyk, gaunt and strange-eyed, came like a moulting eagle to Stark's tent and said:

"Now you must get off your hunkers, Dark Man. You and your Lesser Hearths and your demon hounds. We have broken the path for you. Tread it."

He went back to his camp, angry cat's-paws striking up sand at every flapping step. Halk looked after him.

"That little man makes an evil enemy."

He had spent his idle days creaking and groaning at martial exercises. He had not yet got back his full strength, but half of Halk's strength was greater than most men's. Now he made steel flicker around his head.

"When we enter the city, I'll bear shield beside you."

"Not you," Stark said, "and not Simon, either. If I should fall, there'll be things for you to do."

Stark sent word to the chiefs. He spent time with Ashton. He spent time with Gerrith. He ate and slept, and the day passed.

For Yurunna that night began like the others—as it seemed to the Wandsmen, a year of others, with the whirling winds dancing death around them and over them, and sandy sleeplessness in their smoke-stung eyes, and their limbs aching. Then they began to perceive that there was movement in the darkness.

They tried to follow it. The winds kicked and trampled, blinding them with dust, wreaking havoc along the wall. Twice and thrice the Wandsmen had replaced the defenses of the gate-towers, clearing away scorched wreckage from the square below to give the Yur fighting room. Now again cauldrons and spreading fire were thrown down to smoke and blaze in the square. Gusts of wind pounded at the iron gate, so that it moved with a deep groaning.

Things, said the hounds of Yurunna, where the Houndmaster and two handlers and two apprentice boys held them at the back of the square, away from the fires. *Things come.*

Kill, said the Houndmaster.

The hounds sent fear.

Thirty Tarf, fifteen on a side, bearing a ram made from a green tree trunk cut beside Yurunna's springs, came up the zigzag road to the gate. Twenty more came with them, holding the turtle roof above their heads. They did not flinch from the sending of the hounds.

The hounds said, *Things do not fear us.*

And they became afraid, with a new fear added to the ones they already had, of strange winds and noises and the smell of death.

The Houndmaster said, *Those will come who do.*

He was a tall Wandsman. The tunic under his dented mail was the somber red that marked him next in rank below the Lords Protector. From the time he had been a gray apprentice up from Ged Darod he had

94

lived and worked with Northhounds. He loved them. He loved their ugliness and their savagery. He loved their minds, to which he had become so closely attuned. He loved sharing their simple joy of slaughter. His heart was broken for each hound he had lost to the were-winds.

For the nine traitor hounds he had lost to an off-world monster called Stark, who was neither man nor beast, more than his heart was broken.

The Lords Protector had come, the august and holy men he had served all his life, tending the hounds and training them and sending them north to guard the Citadel from all intruders. His hounds—his hounds!—had not guarded, had betrayed, had followed after this sky-born blasphemy who flouted their power; and the Citadel was a burnt-out ruin, the Lords Protector driven shamefully to seek refuge at Yurunna.

They had been kind. They had absolved him of fault. Still, the hounds were his.

The dishonor was his.

After the Lords Protector, Gelmar came, in such haste that he killed his beast within sight of the gate. The Ochar were broken. Yurunna stood alone against the host of the north, and the leader of that host was Stark, with his nine faithless hounds.

Gelmar and the Lords Protector had fled on, down the road to Ged Darod. Now, as they had feared, Yurunna was tottering to its fall. And the Houndmaster had seen from the battlements a big dark man on a dappled beast riding a circuit of the walls, with nine white hounds running by him.

He spoke to his own hounds, the twenty-four that were all he had left, and less than half of them full-grown. He spoke to them gently, because the young ones trembled.

Wait, he said. *There will yet be killing.*

The ram begin to swing. The deep drum-sound beat out heavily over Yurunna.

Muster-horns blew, calling the Yur to defend the gate.

The defenses along the wall, already thin, were

thinned still more. Many of the storerooms were gutted, and the emplacements destroyed. Because of the blocking of streets where fire and wind had brought down buildings, bodies of men could no longer be moved quickly back and forth. They could only move freely on the wall. Now many of those who manned it were drawn to the gate.

When the wind dropped, it was seen that masses of men had gathered in the plain below and were already on the zigzag road.

Stark was under the wall with his hounds and fifty Tarf, led by Klatlekt. Half the Fallarin, with the rest of the Tarf and one-third of the tribal army, waited in the fields.

Kill, said Stark. *Clear the wall.*

The hounds ranged on either side, sending fear to the Yur above.

When the chosen section of the wall was cleared, the Fallarin hop-flapped up the sheer cliff, up the unscalable wall, and made fast ropes of twisted hide around the crenels of the firestep.

Tarf swarmed up the ropes, swords and shields hung at their backs. Some spread out to hold the wall. Others hauled up rope ladders or helped the tribesmen climb.

Stark forced the growling hounds to submit while he fitted slings under their bellies. The Tarf hauled them up, careless of their rage and fear. Stark climbed beside them. On either side now came red Kref and green Thorn.

The Fallarin returned to their mounts and rode away.

On the broad top of the wall Stark gathered his party: Klatlekt and twenty Tarf and the hounds. He set out toward the gate.

The hounds forgot the indignity of the slings. There was a dark excitement in their minds, a wildness mixed with fear.

Many minds, N'Chaka. Too many. All hate. All red. Red. Red.

96

In the square, where the ram was a wincing thunder in their ears, the hounds of Yurunna said:

Things come. There along wall. And men. And hounds.

Hounds?

Yes.

The Houndmaster stroked rough heads. *Good,* he said. *That is good.*

He passed word to the Wandsman captains that invaders were on the wall. He snapped orders to his two handlers and the apprentice boys, all Wandsmen, though of lesser and least rank, and thus safe like himself from the Northhounds. All were leaden with weariness, and the boys were all but useless with fright. However, the time would not be long. They would do.

He did not call up any of the Yur. The renegade hounds would only kill them before they could shoot arrow or lift spear, and the captains would need every one.

He spoke to his favorite hound, an old wise bitch.

Hounds, Mika.

Mika made an eager growling and led the way.

Up on the wall Gerd said suddenly, *N'Chaka. They come to kill.*

16

Stark had come far enough around the curve of the wall to be able to see the top of the north gate-tower above the roofs. The tribesmen were coming strongly behind him, pouring up onto the wall, helped by the strong arms of the Tarf. They could still be thrown back if the hounds of Yurunna spread death and terror among them.

Stark went down stone steps, down off the wall, into

the street below. Klatlekt and the twenty Tarf came with him.

The hounds slunk, whining.

Houndmaster, Gerd said. *Angry.*

Dim faint memories stirred, of old days, of running in couples with littermates, of an overmastering mind that gave orders and engendered a respect that was as near to love as a Northhound could feel.

He will kill us, Grith said.

How?

With hounds. With his great sword.

Kill N'Chaka, Gerd said.

Not N'Chaka, Stark answered. And, contemptuously, *Stay, then, if you fear the Houndmaster. N'Chaka will fight for you.*

N'Chaka understood that he had little choice about fighting in any case. That was why the Tarf were there. But he felt a responsibility toward these fangy horrors who had become his allies. He had deliberately seduced them into betraying their masters, knowing that they could not comprehend what they were doing. They had followed him, they had served him, they were his. He had a duty to fight for them.

To the Tarf he said, "Do not touch mine."

He set off along a street that led inward from the wall. He had no worry about finding the hounds of Yurunna. They would find him. He wanted it to be as far as possible from the tribesmen.

Gerd howled. Then he bayed, and Grith bayed, and the others took it up. They followed Stark, and that deep and dreadful challenge rang ahead of them along the silent stony ways with no other sound in them but the drumbeat of the ram.

The hounds of Yurunna heard. The young ones whined, partly from fear and partly from excitement, feeling a new ferocity rise within them. The old ones lifted their own voices, and their eyes glowed with a deadly light. The old relationship was long forgotten. These were strangers invading their territory, crying a pack cry, following a strange leader who was neither hound nor Wandsman.

The Houndmaster said kill. They would kill gladly.

The streets were not too much encumbered. The stout stone buildings here had resisted the winds and fires. Both parties moved rapidly, hound-minds guiding eagerly toward a meeting.

The Houndmaster knew the streets, and Stark did not.

The Houndmaster spoke. Handlers and struggling apprentices forced the hounds to a reluctant halt. Ahead of them was a small open space, a little square where four streets met.

The Houndmaster waited.

In that one of the four streets that led from the wall, Gerd said, *There!* and rushed ahead into the square.

Nine hounds running, heads down, backs a-bristle. 'N'Chaka would have held them. But N'Chaka was fighting his own fight.

When the Northhounds fought each other, as the males did for leadership of the pack, they used every weapon they had. Fear would not kill a Northhound, but it served as a whip to wound and drive, the stronger against the weaker. The hounds of Yurunna did not at first send fear against the invading hounds. By order of the Houndmaster they sent it all against the alien leader.

N'Chaka struggled to stand erect, to breathe.

To live.

"Slip them," said the Houndmaster, and the hounds of Yurunna went free.

Twenty-four against nine, in the small square. Twenty-four encircling and overlapping nine, carrying them back by sheer weight into the mouth of the street whence they had come. Twenty-four and nine inextricably mixed. To the Tarf, indistinguishable.

The Houndmaster followed them with his great sword raised high, and to him each hound was as well known as the hairs and scars and pits upon his own face.

Three hounds of Yurunna, with the Houndmaster's old bitch Mika leading, burst out of the boiling mass into the street where the Tarf stood crammed between the walls, their effective force reduced by the constriction to no more than five or six.

At their forefront Klatlekt stood by Stark, blinking his green-gold eyes.

He warded the enemy hounds' first rush with his sword, while Stark sobbed for breath and stared blindly with the icy sweat beading his face.

"We must have fighting room," said Klatlekt. Houndfear could not harm him. The fangs and the ripping claws could. He plucked at Stark with one powerful hand. "Come. Or we go without you."

The hounds attacked again, two feinting to draw Klatlekt's blade, the bitch driving straight for Stark's throat.

In the square the sword of the Houndmaster flashed down. And up. And down again.

N'Chaka saw death coming, smelled death, heard it. Sheer brute reflex, the dangerous last blind outlashing, brought his own sword forward.

Houndmaster! Kill, Gerd! Kill, Or we all die.

The Houndmaster, untouchable Wandsman belly deep in hounds, swung his sword.

Gerd, torn and bleeding, with N'Chaka's cry ringing in his mind, saw the flash of that blade above him and broke the unbreakable commandment.

The Yurunna bitch-hound shrieked, an almost human sound, as the life-long mind-bond snapped. She turned her head, searching, crying out, and Stark ran her through the neck, clumsy and vicious with the black terror on him.

He went forward, shouting to his hounds, and they flung themselves in a frenzy of guilt and triumph on the hounds of Yurunna, sensing that the Houndmaster's death had robbed them of their strength.

The guilding presence was gone, the strong firm voice that had spoken in their minds since they first saw light.

Stark became that voice.

Go back to your kennel. Back, or we kill.

The hounds of Yurunna begged help from the

handlers. The handlers no longer spoke. Gerd had learned how easy it was to kill Wandsmen.

Back to your kennel! Go!

The apprentices had fled long ago. The hounds of Yurunna were quite alone. The strangers and their strange leader fought fiercely. The things fought with them, the unhuman things that wielded long sharp swords and were not touched by fear.

Go, said the strong commanding voice in their minds.

The young hounds, already fearful and with no master to give them courage, did as Stark told them. There were eight still able to run.

The old hounds died there, full of rage and grief, and Stark knew that if the Houndmaster had been present on the Plain of Worldheart, he would never have made himself leader of Flay's pack.

The small square fell quiet again. Gerd and Grith came panting to Stark's side. Only three others came with them, and not one unmarked. Stark and Klatlekt and several more of the Tarf had taken wounds, but none was disabled.

Klatlekt blinked heavy eyelids and said, "If this is finished, we will return to the wall."

"It is finished," Stark said, knowing that more than this fight was finished. The face of the Houndmaster stared white and accusing from amid the rough sprawled carcasses. As a terror and a menace, as a weapon of the Wandsmen, the Northhounds were finished forever.

Stark took Gerd's head between his hands. *You have killed Wandsmen.*

Gerd's teeth showed, even though he trembled. *Houndmaster killed us.*

So. Other Wandsmen will kill.

With a strange echo of despair, Gerd said, *We kill them.*

Grith?

We kill.

Come, then, Stark said, and went off after the quick-footed Tarf, who had not waited for him. He was con-

101

scious of his hurts and of his weariness, but he was exhilarated by this triumph over the Wandsmen. He ran swiftly, his heart beating hot, eager for more.

The booming of the ram had stopped. In its place was the confused uproar of men fighting. The tribesmen were making their attack.

Most of them had come down off the wall to strike the Yur in the streets and the square. A strong party of tribesmen and Tarf had gone on to the tower and were fighting their way into it. Down below it housed the mechanism that controlled the gate, which was standing firm in spite of the battering.

Stark and his hounds lent aid where it would help the most. He took a particular pleasure in picking out the Wandsman captains and saying, *Kill.* It was time they felt the weight of the weapon they had used for so long against other men.

The north tower was taken. The clanking mechanism hauled open the iron gate, and the tide of purple and white, brown and yellow, poured through it into the square. The zigzag road was a solid river of men rushing upward, yelping, howling, brandishing sword and spear, and below the road more men came from among the warty crops and spiny orchards to jostle for a place.

Nothing could stand against that tide. The bodies of tribesmen spitted on Yur spears hung there with no room to fall. The defenders were forced back, back against stone walls, out of the square, into the streets, where the bands of Hann and Marag, Kref and Thuran, Thorn and yellow Qard hunted them and killed.

When the killing was done, the looting began. Most of the fat storehouses where food and drink were kept had escaped the damage of the werewinds, being in the heart of the occupied section of Yurunna; many of them were in underground chambers cut in the rock. The tribesmen pillaged the storerooms, and the houses, and the public places. The Keepers of the six Hearths did what they could to maintain order.

Even so, things happened.

The men found the great walled house of the Yur

women and battered down its doors. Instead of the orgy of pleasure they had anticipated, they found creatures like obscene white slugs that stared at them with empty eyes and screamed without ceasing, clutching their unnatural young like so many identical blank-faced dolls. Overcome with disgust, the tribesmen made a silence in the place and never once thought of these degraded things as food.

That was the end of the Yur, the Well-Created servants of the Wandsmen. Some of the men still lived, but there would be no more breeding.

Stark had no part in this. He had gone to the kennels.

The gray-clad apprentices were there, boys up from Ged Darod only that year. One of them, a sullen heavy-faced youth, was crouched in a corner hugging himself and waiting to die, with hate and fear and nothing else at all in his eyes.

The other was with the hounds. He was slight and dark, his boy's face still unformed, his boy's hands too large and knuckly. He was afraid. There was no reason why he should not be. He was hollow-eyed and red-eyed and pale with exhaustion. But he was with the hounds where he belonged. And he met Stark's gaze with what dignity he could muster, even though he knew that those five grim blood-dabbled beasts at Stark's heels might kill him where he stood.

"How are you called?" Stark asked.

"Tuchvar," said the boy. And again, more clearly, "Tuchvar."

"Where from?"

"Tregad."

Tregad was a city-state, east of Irnan and north of Ged Darod.

Stark nodded and turned to the young hounds. They whined and glanced at him furtively with their hellhound eyes that had not yet come to their full evil brightness.

You know me.

They did.

I am N'Chaka. I lead you now.

The hounds appealed to Tuchvar. *Houndmaster?* They knew that that mind had ceased to speak to them. They could not yet grasp the fact that it would never speak again.

Tuchvar said aloud, "This man is master now."

N'Chaka? Master?

Master, Stark said. *These old ones will teach you the law.*

Gerd moved forward, stiff-legged and growling. The young hounds said, *We will obey.*

Stark spoke now to Gerd and Grith. *Will you go with me below Yurunna?*

It was their turn to be uneasy. *Not know. Hound-kind never sent but to Citadel.*

Stark said, *You cannot stay here. Things with swords will kill you, things that do not feel fear. You must go with me.*

Go with N'Chaka or die?

Yes.

Then we go.

Good.

He didn't know whether it was good or not. They were cold-weather beasts, and he had no idea how well they would adjust to warmer climates. Some animals managed very well. In any case what he told them was true. Neither the Fallarin nor the Lesser Hearths of Kheb would consent to having a pack of Northhounds loose and leaderless to prey on them and their cattle. The Tarf would see to that.

Gelmar and the Lords Protector had not counted on the Tarf.

He explained all this to Tuchvar. "Will you come with the hounds, as least as far as Tregad? Or do you serve the Wandsmen too loyally?"

"Not," said Tuchvar carefully, "so loyally that I want to die for them right here." He had been listening to the sounds outside and not liking them. He did not see what good it would do for him to die. It could not help the Wandsmen. It would certainly not help him.

The other apprentice spoke up from his corner, voice pitched high with fear and spite.

"He serves no one loyally but the hounds. Even at Ged Darod he was thinking all the time about starships and other worlds and listening to the heresies of Pedrallon."

Stark went over and yanked him to his feet.

"Stop shivering, boy. Nobody's going to kill you. What's your name?"

"Varik. From Ged Darod." Pride stirred in the lumpish face. "I was born there, at the Refuge."

"Farer's get," said Tuchvar. "They haven't any fathers."

"The Lords Protector are my fathers," said Varik, "and better than yours, sitting fat behind walls and trying to hide away food from the hungry."

"My father's dead," said Tuchvar bitterly, "but at least I know who he was, and he worked."

"All right," said Stark. "Now. Who is Pedrallon?"

"A red Wandsman," said Varik, "with the rank of Coordinator. The Twelve took away his rank and put him to doing penance for a year. It was supposed to be a secret, of course; they said Pedrallon had been relieved of his duties because of his health, but nothing stays a secret in our dormitories, not for very long."

Busy little apprentice Wandsmen, Stark thought, nibbling up crumbs of forbidden gossip like mice in a cupboard.

"What was his heresy?"

Tuchvar answered.

"He said the migrations were beginning again. He said that some of Skaith's people would have to go, to make room for others. He said it was wrong to stop the Irnanese."

17

There was a complex of buildings where the two score Wandsmen had lived, with such women as they might have from time to time. The quarters lacked nothing of comfort. Stark and his party and the Keepers of the six Hearths had lodged themselves here. The Fallarin, ever exclusive, had found themselves another place.

At the center of the complex was a wide hall furnished with handsome things brought up from the south. The Hearth-Keepers had managed to keep their men from looting here. Rich carpets were on the floor. Hangings brightened the dark stone of the walls. Many lamps lighted it, in a profligate squandering of oil. Braziers gave off warmth. Tarf and tribesmen mingled, carrying food and wine to the tables, where the conquerors of Yurunna were celebrating their victory.

The hall was crowded. Everyone who could possibly force his way in had done so. They stuffed themselves on the plenty of the Wandsmen's storerooms, washing it down with Southron wine and bitter beer. When the feasting was done, some of the men danced with flashing swords while drums thumped and pipes shrilled. Others rose and sang boasting songs. They began to drink to their leaders, each Hearth vying with the others in claims to bravery and prowess in battle.

They drank to the Fallarin.

They drank to the Dark Man.

Ildann put down his goblet and said, "Now Yurunna is taken, we remember your promise, Stark."

He spoke so that the words were a challenge, intended to be heard by all. He waited until the hall became quiet, with every head bent toward him, listening, and then he asked:

"What will you do now?"

Stark smiled. "Have no fear, Ildann. You have Yurunna. I leave to you and your fellows the task of sharing out the loot and the land, the placing of villages and the method of ruling them. You're at full liberty to kill each other if you choose. I've done my part."

"You go south, then?"

"To Tregad. To raise an army for Irnan. If we succeed, there will be war with the Wandsmen." He looked out over the hall, at all the masked faces. "War. Loot. High pay. And at the end, the starships. The freedom of the stars. That may mean nothing to you. If so, stay and make bricks for the villages. If any wish to come with me, you will be welcome."

Ildann had three sons. The youngest rose to his feet. His name was Sabak. He was slender as a reed and light as a roebuck in his movements, and he had fought well. He said:

"I will go with you, Dark Man."

Ildann crashed his fist on the table. "No!"

Sabak said, "I have a mind to see these ships, Father."

"Why? What do you want with other worlds? Have I not fought to bring you the best of this one? Yurunna, boy! We have taken Yurunna!"

"And that is well, Father. I too fought. Now I wish to see the ships."

"You're a child," said Ildann, suddenly quiet. "Men must feed and breed wherever they are. One world or another, feeding and breeding are the most of a man's life, along with the fighting that goes with them. No matter where you go, you'll find nothing better than what you have."

"That may be, Father. But I will see for myself."

Ildann turned on Stark, and Gerd, crouched by Stark's feet, sprang up snarling.

"I see now why the Wandsmen wish to kill you," Ildann said. "You bring a poison with you. You have poisoned my son with dreams."

107

A puff of wind made the lamps flicker. Alderyk had risen. The light gleamed gold at his throat and waist and in his falcon eyes.

"The boy has wisdom enough to understand that there is something beyond the walls of his sty, Ildann. Feeding and breeding are not enough for everyone. I too will go with the Dark Man. I am a king, and I have a duty to be as wise as Ildann's youngest son."

There was a clamor of voices. Ildann shouted furiously.

Again the lamps flickered and the cloaks of the men rustled as the small wind admonished them.

"The ships are there," Alderyk said. "The men are there, men from other worlds. We cannot pretend that things are still as they were before the landing, or ever will be again. We must know, we must learn." He paused. "There is another matter."

He spoke now to Stark, his eyes agleam with cruel mirth.

"I said you were like a black whirling wind, to break and shatter. It's our world you blow across, Dark Man, and when you fly away among the stars, we'll be left to deal with whatever wreckage you may have devised. So it seems my duty to be with you."

A buffet of air slapped Stark about the head, tossing his hair, making him blink and turn aside.

"I control winds, you know," said Alderyk.

Stark nodded tranquilly. "Very well." He stood up. "Let the word be passed. I leave Yurunna tomorrow, when Old Sun is at his highest. Let every man who wishes to come south with me be in the square beside the gate at that time, mounted, armed and with three week's provisions."

He left the hall, with Ildann's angry voice raised again behind him. Ashton came, too, and Halk and Gerrith.

Halk said, "I think I'll go into the streets and drum up trade." In the quiet of the corridor, the sounds of celebration came clearly from outside. Through the windows Stark could see fires burning and men moving about them, dancing, chanting, drinking. Grith and the three rose stiffly from where they had lain on watch.

"Take Gerd with you to watch your back," Stark said. "The Hearth-Keepers may object to this stealing of their men."

"Keep your grimhound," Halk said, and touched his sword. "This is enough."

"Will you argue?" Stark asked, and Gerd swung his heavy head to stare at Halk.

Halk shrugged. He walked away. Gerd followed. Halk did not look back or notice him.

"What will you get?" Ashton asked.

"A few boys like Sabak, with stars in their eyes. Malcontents, troublemakers, the restless types who would rather fight than make bricks. Not too many, probably." He smiled briefly. "Alderyk I'll be glad to have, in spite of his thorns."

He said good night and went to his quarters. He sat for a time, brooding. He knew that Gerrith would be waiting for him. He did not go to her. Instead, he took a lamp and made his way quietly, with the hounds, along the chilly corridors and down several flights of steps until he reached the cellars, cut deep into the rock. The Wandsmen had had no need of prison cells and so there were none. Some of the smaller storage chambers had been pressed into service as dungeons, to hold the handful of Wandsmen who had survived the fall of Yurunna.

Half a dozen of the yellow-cloaked Qard were lounging on piles of grain sacks, by way of being guards. Two of them played a game with varicolored pebbles, tossing them into a space marked out with intricate patterns drawn in the dust of the floor. The others made bets.

One of them looked up. "Hey," he said. "The Hound-master!"

They all left off what they were doing and stood. Stark stared at them with displeasure.

"How long have you called me by that name?"

"Since we first heard it from the Hann, who first saw

you with the Northhounds," said one of the men. "Didn't you know?"

"No. What else am I called?"

"Herder of Runners. Dark Man. Some even call you Starborn, but most of us don't believe that."

"Ah," said Stark. "You don't."

The man shrugged. "It may be. But it's easier to think that you came from the south."

"What do you know of the south?"

"There are great cities there, as high as mountains, and forests between them where there are all sorts of monsters and the trees eat men. Old Sun burns there with great heat, which is itself unnatural. I think anything might come from the south."

"Well," said Stark, "in a manner of speaking, I did come from there. What will you do now that you have Yurunna?"

"Build a village." The city was too large, too dark and cheerless for the tribesmen. They would build in the familiar pattern, at the edge of cultivation, close to their fields and herds. "We'll bring our women to tend the crops; men can't do that, you know. The land bears only for women. It is the same in the south?"

"I can name you a dozen places where it's so, and another dozen where it isn't." And not only in the south, friend, Stark thought. All over the galaxy.

The man shook his head. "You and your companions are the only strangers I've ever seen. There are different thoughts behind your eyes. I hadn't ever wondered about people living and thinking in other ways. Our way seems the only one, the only *right* one . . ."

One of the other men leaned forward. "Say truly, Dark Man. Are you from the south, or from another world?"

"From another world," said Stark. "Look up into the sky some night and see the stars; think of the ships going back and forth between them. Maybe some day you'll get tired of fighting the cold and the Runners and decide to go out there yourselves."

The men muttered and glanced at each other.

"We are Qard," said the first man. "We have a place in the tribe, we have a set of laws to live by. If we went to some other place . . ."

" 'The land shapes us,' " Stark said. " 'If we were in another place, we would be another people.' " He remembered Kazimni, the wolf-eyed Izvandian, captain of mercenaries at Irnan, who had said that. "And of course it's true. Yet there are those who have lived for centuries with the hope that someday the star-roads would be open."

He remembered the ruins of the towers away in the darklands, and the madness of Hargoth the Corn King, who had seen the ships in his Winter Dreaming, shining beside the sea. He and his people had been ready to migrate all the long way south to Skeg, singing the Hymn of Deliverance, to find those ships. They had hailed Stark as the savior come to lead them, until that black day at Thyra and Gelmar's cruel lie. The Corn King and his priests had left there stricken men, believing that the ships were already gone and that their endless waiting must continue.

"Anyway," said the tribesman, "the ships are far away, if they exist at all. The choice will not be made in my lifetime."

And perhaps not in mine either, Stark thought, and said, "I will speak to the red Wandsman."

There was only one of that rank among the survivors. His name was Clain, and he had been one of the administrators of the city. He was intelligent and well controlled; a rather cold and rigid man, too proud to show the rage and despair he must be feeling. Which was not true of the lesser Wandsmen. They were all to be kept alive with a view to ransom or as possible trade goods in future negotiations.

Clain was alone, at his own request, and not uncomfortable in his confinement. He stood when Stark entered, stiff with unwelcome, looking bitterly at the hounds. Stark left the three outside, taking only Grith with him into the cell. He shut the heavy door.

"Can you not leave me in peace?" the Wandsman asked, and Stark felt sorry for him in a way. Battered,

111

exhausted and soiled, Clain was the model of painful defeat.

"I've already told you that Irnan still fights. I've told you all I know about what forces have been sent against her. I've told you there was talk among the Lords Protector, in their short visit here, concerning the starport at Skeg . . ."

"They spoke of closing the starport if Irnan should be relieved and the revolt widened."

"I told you that."

"They are guarding the starport closely, hoping that my friend and I may come there."

"I told you that, too."

Stark shrugged. "We knew it anyway. Now tell me about Pedrallon."

Clain sighed. "I have told you that I don't know Pedrallon."

"He's a red Wandsman. Surely there aren't so many of you at Ged Darod that you haven't at least heard of him."

"My place was not at Ged Darod, it was here . . ."

"One of your colleagues has told us that you went down to Ged Darod eight months ago, at about the time Pedrallon was disciplined by the Twelve."

"That's true. But I am not in the confidence of the Twelve."

"Really. Yet the gray apprentices knew all about it."

Clain's mouth made an icy pretense of a smile. "I suggest that you return to the kennels, then, for further information."

Stark frowned. "You have no idea of the basis of Pedrallon's heresy?"

"I am not concerned with such matters. I went to Ged Darod to see about increasing the supplies we send—did send—to the Ochar. Their crops have suffered . . ."

"You don't know why he was disciplined so severely?"

"I only heard that he was ill."

"And you don't know what his penance was?"

"I told you—"

112

"Yes," said Stark, "you did indeed. Grith . . ."

All this time Clain had been avoiding the sight of the Northhound, as though he knew what must happen because of her. Now his skin became even grayer than before.

"I beg you—"

"I believe you do," said Stark. "I'm sorry." *Grith, touch. Not kill. Touch.*

The massive head lifted. Stark could have sworn she smiled, pulling her dark lips back from gleaming fangs. Her bright eyes grew brighter still, smoky fires under heavy brows.

Clain went on his knees and wept. "They were our servants," he said between chattering jaws. "Ours. This is evil. Wrong."

Touch him, Grith.

In no more than five minutes Stark had everything he wanted.

He left Clain curled up, shivering on his pallet. He nodded to the Qard and went up the stairs again. He knocked at Ashton's door and went into the room.

Noises filtered through the shuttered windows from the streets of Yurunna. The tribesmen were still joyful. Ashton looked at Stark's face and sighed.

"What have you found out?"

"Pedrallon was sentenced to a year of menial duties at the Refuge as well as being stripped of his rank. They seem to have considered executing him, but didn't—Wandsmen are hardly ever sentenced to death. The small number of Wandsmen who openly supported his position were also punished, in lesser ways. There may have been others who were not open."

"Well?" said Ashton.

"Pedrallon was accused of being in secret communication with the star-captains at Skeg. He denied it. He was also accused of having a group of adherents on the outside. He denied that, too. If there was a conspiracy, it was a small one, and it may be out of business entirely. But from what Clain said, there is a possibility that Pedrallon had secured a transceiver from one of the captains and that some of his group

113

had it hidden in or near Ged Darod. If so, it's still there. The Wandsmen never found it."

"A transceiver," Ashton said, and sighed again.

"If the Wandsmen send the ships away, as they promise to do, we'll be cutting our own throats if we succeed in raising men at Tregad. If we don't, if you and I just run for Skeg, our chances of getting through their cordon are about nil."

"Do you know there's a transceiver?"

"I said it's a possibility."

"Ged Darod. The heart and center. And you're thinking of going there."

"I don't think there's any way out of it," Stark said, "if we hope to leave Skaith alive. Or dead."

18

The Wandsmen's Road was old. Above Ged Darod it ran through the barren places where survival was difficult, so that even during the Wandering and the unsettled times that followed, the road had not been too much exposed to attack by marauding bands. The system of wayhouses made travel on the road swift and comfortable for those authorized to use it. For the unauthorized, it was death.

Over the centuries there had been much coming and going along the road: Wandsmen and their armed escorts and mercenaries on the Lower Road, Yur and Ochar above; caravans bringing goods and supplies up to Yurunna, with their escorts and companies of lower-grade Wandsmen; caravans bringing women for the Wandsmen at Yurunna and for the distant peoples of Thyra and the Towers, beyond the mountains in the haunted darklands. Special parties, outwardly indistinguishable from the ordinary, conveyed each new

Lord Protector north to the Citadel, which he would never leave until in his turn he was laid to rest among the thermal pits of Worldheart. But never had there been such a company on the road as went upon it now from Yurunna.

Stark rode at the head, on a dappled beast. Thirteen great white hounds followed him, with the gray apprentice Tuchvar to whip them in. With Stark at the head of the column were Ashton and Gerrith, and Halk with a great sword slung at his back, the hilt standing up over his shoulder; somewhere in the storerooms of Yurunna he had found a blade to his liking for size and weight. Alderyk rode where he would, Klatlekt and half a dozen Tarf trotting attendance beside him.

Next were fifty Fallarin, with their rich harness shining and dust in the folds of their wings, and five score Tarf with their four-handed swords and curiously stubby bows from which they could fire a deadly stream of arrows.

After them came the tribesmen, purple Hann with Sabak at their head, red Kref and green Thorn, white Thuran and yellow Qard, brown Marag, all in dusty leather. One hundred and eighty-seven of them, divided into groups according to their tribe, the day's place in line of each group chosen by lot in the morning. Stark hoped that they would become a single body of fighting men, but that time was not yet. He humored their pride.

South from Yurunna, at the great scarp of the Edge, the mountain wall on their right hand came to an end. Four thousand feet below, the desert spread away to the horizon without a break, except for abrupt upthrusting fangs of rock, worn thin with endless gnawing at the wind. The sand was streaked and stained in many colors, black and rust red, poison green, sulphur yellow. It was chillingly devoid of life, but the markers of the road marched out across it, a line of tiny dots.

At the foot of the Edge, just below them, where springs ran from beneath the cliffs, there were patches of cultivation and areas where a brownish sward covered the sand. A multitude of speckles on these areas were the herd-beasts of Yurunna, which had been driven to pasture here out of the way of the army. Men would come presently to drive them back.

The company wound its way down a steep and tortuous road cut in the sheer rock.

It was warmer at the foot of the scarp. The smell of water was strong in the dry air. High above the fields, where the face of the cliff was eroded into open caves, inaccessible dwellings squatted in remoteness and mystery; clusters of uneven walls with inscrutable windows at which no faces showed. Whether or not the star-roads were open made little difference here.

The company refilled waterskins at the springs and went on.

They moved swiftly, yet the desert seemed to have no boundaries. The way houses had been abandoned, beasts driven off, supplies carried away or destroyed. By this they knew that spies had been left to watch Yurunna, and that word its fall had gone ahead of them. The wells had been blocked with boulders or choked with sand. Water supplies ran short. Men sickened of the hard stony waste with its deathly colors like the skin of a poisonous reptile. The beasts became footsore. There began to be grumbling and discontent. The hounds panted in the warmer air and the tribesmen threw open their leather cloaks. The Fallarin sulked and wished for water to wash their fur glossy again.

As Stark had guessed, most of the tribesmen were the restless ones, the trouble makers, and the Hearth-Keepers had not been too sorry to see them gone. At night Stark went among them, talking to them, telling tales of marches and battles on worlds far away, imbuing them with as much of his own strength of purpose as was possible, binding them to himself by sheer force of personality.

Nevertheless, he watched them.

Gerd roused him one night. A dozen or so hooded forms were stealing away from the camp, on foot, leading their animals. Stark let them get a certain distance away and then sent the pack. The deserters came crawling back to camp herded by thirteen grim white hounds. The attempt was not repeated.

Yet Stark could not blame them. Sometimes at night he stood, with Gerd and Grith by him, and listened to the stillness and felt the empty leagues around him and wondered what he was leading his small legion into. If they survived this ugly desolation, their way to Tregad was by no means clear. Gelmar had a long head start. Gelmar would have the news from Yurunna. Gelmar would look at a map, consider the logistics and assume that Tregad, being the nearest possible source of help for Irnan, would be Stark's most likely destination. Surely he would think of some way to intercept him.

They were three days without water at the last. Then they came to the first stream, with a line of stunted trees twisting along its course, and knew that they would live.

Stark had brought maps from Yurunna. As soon as was possible he left the Wandsmen's Road and struck out southeast for Tregad.

The land was not hospitable. In the Barrens to the west there had at least been an abundance of water and edible mosses for the beasts. Here there was little in the way of forage except along the stingy watercourses. Still, the beasts were hardy and they managed, and the men grew more cheerful even though their own bellies were pinched. The deathly colors had been replaced by an honest gray-brown. The Fallarin splashed and fluttered like birds at the cold pools and sleeked their fur until it glistened. The hounds had remained well so far. Here they hunted and found game, small shy creatures that might outrun the hounds' feet but not their fear.

The Three Ladies now ruled the sky again, glorious clusters brighter than moons, so that the nights were filled with a milky radiance. To Stark and the Irnanese they were like old friends. To the Fallarin and the tribesmen they were an astonishment.

117

With startling abruptness the nature of the country changed. They came out of the barren places and into the northern edge of the Fertile Belt not far above the latitude of Irnan. Here were grass and water and arable land.

Here, for the first time, they found villages, walled, dourly squatting above their fields, with watchtowers here and there to guard against predators—chiefly, the Wild Bands.

Several times the hounds gave warning. Stark and his men could catch glimpses of them, furtive slinking forms all hair and tatters, loping along at a distance, eyeing them.

Sabak said, "They're no better than Runners."

"Not much," Stark agreed, "but some. They're not as brainless, they haven't got such big teeth and they're not anything like as fast." He added, "Don't straggle."

Using the hounds and the Tarf as scouts, Stark was able to hit the villages before they could shut their gates. At each one he spoke to the people. The Dark Man of the prophecy told them of the fall of the Citadel and of the taking of Yurunna. They were a small dark people here, quite different from the tall Irnanese, and their manner was not friendly. Yet when they heard of the news their faces brightened. They too chafed under the yoke of the Wandsmen, who came at every harvest time to take a portion of their meager crops so that they were always on the edge of hunger. Many of the people had gone, to become Farers. Slowly the villages were dying. The hardness of the life and the small rewards had left ruins here and there and fields abandoned to the greedy weeds.

In each village a few of the folk picked up what arms they had or could improvise, and they joined with Stark's company. And along the paths and the herdsmen's tracks and the hunters' ways, messengers took the words of the Dark Man among scattered settlements.

Other messengers were abroad, too.

One night a signal fire flared atop a distant hill, its

118

light paled by the lovely glow of the Three Ladies. A second fire kindled to life farther away, and then a third, a tiny pinpoint. The fourth Stark could not see, but he knew it was there, and a fifth—as many as were needed.

"They've seen us," Halk said. "They know where we are and where we're going. Wherever they choose to be waiting for us, there they will wait."

Stark found the main road to Tregad, and the company went down it like a thunderbolt.

It had been spring when Stark and his companions left these latitudes, with orchards just in blossom and the fresh green blanketing the fields. Now grain was yellowing toward harvest and fruit was heavy on the boughs.

Deep summer. Yet there was no one but themselves on the road to Tregad, where there ought to have been traders and drovers, wandering mountebanks and the bands of Farers. The gates of the villages they passed hung open, but the people had gone to hide themselves in the hills and the fields were untended.

Stark, with the hounds and some of the Tarf, scouted ahead, alert for ambush.

The hounds were not as tireless as they had once been. The young ones especially had become thin and listless. They suffered from fluxes, and Tuchvar worried and nursed them with infusions of herbs and green bark from a particular shrub. The old hounds fared better, though they suffered in the midday heat, mild as it was in this temperate climate. Still, they went obediently as they were told, and Stark rode with them far in advance of the troop.

There was no ambush. Woods and narrow defiles held no enemy.

"But of course," said Ashton, "Gelmar knows you've got the hounds, so an ambush wouldn't work—they'd warn you."

"He must meet us somewhere," Halk said. "He or his people."

"No doubt they will," said Stark.

119

And they did.

Tregad, when they came to it in the middle of an afternoon, was a city much like Irnan, stone-built and solid behind massive walls. Irnan was gray; the stone of Tregad was honey-colored so that it appeared far less grim, glowing warmly in the sunlight with the broad fields and orchards at its feet and its head half-way up the shoulder of a mountain, and a wide dark lake beyond.

Four thousand Farers thronged the fields and orchards. They trampled the standing crops into the ground, tore the fruiting branches from the trees. They howled and screamed and surged in irregular waves upon the gates of the city, which were shut against them.

There were some scraps of color on the city wall just below the battlements. Stark made out the bodies of six men hanging there, one in a red tunic, five in green.

"It looks," he said, "as if Tregad has hung up her Wandsmen."

Halk's great blade came rasping from its sheath. His face, still gaunt and craggy, shone with exultation.

"Tregad has revolted, then! Well, Dark Man, there are allies beyond that Farer trash! What will you do? Attack? Or run away?"

19

Halk leaned forward, his jaw thrust out, challenging. Stark had an idea that if he said run, the long blade would be for him.

Farer trash or not, the odds were staggering. He did not know what had happened in Tregad, though he could make a guess. Presumably, having slain their

Wandsmen for whatever reason, the people of the city were committed to revolt. Presumably, when they saw a small force attacking the Farers, they would make a sally to support it. If they did not, or if they came too late, the results would be unpleasant.

Stark sighed and said, "Alderyk?"

The Fallarin had been staring at the mob, his aristocratic nose wrinkling with disgust.

"I think we must have a wind," he said, "to blow away the stink."

He rode back to his people. They began to move out, forming the familiar crescent—a much smaller one this time, and with no Runners ahead of it to drive against the enemy. Stark sent Tuchvar with Grith and half of the pack to stay by Gerrith and Ashton, both of whom were armed and ready. He himself rode back along the line, snapping orders.

The Farers began to be aware of the newcomers.

They were drawn from every race of the Fertile Belt, in all colors, sizes and shapes. They were of all ages, except young children and the very old. They were dressed, or not dressed, in every conceivable fashion, each according to his taste; rags, body-paint, flowing things, flapping things, no things. Some were shaven bald as eggs, others had hair to their knees. Some were adorned with flowers or plucked branches hung with fruit. Some affected tufts of leaves, or feathers or garlands of the potent love-weed. These were the blessed children of the Lords Protector, the weak to be succored, the homeless to be sheltered, the hungry to be fed. Happy children, blowing free with the winds of the world, living only for the day because the years of Old Sun were numbered and there was no time to waste on anything but love and joy.

Their other name was mob.

The ones in the outer fields saw Stark's troop first. They stopped their trampling and stared. The stopping and staring spread gradually inward toward the wall, until the whole motley crowd of them had fallen quiet.

They stared across a level space of turf at the company that had appeared so suddenly from among the

121

low hills above Tregad. They saw the dark man on the dappled beast, the huge white hounds, Halk and the sun-haired woman and the off-world man, the winged Fallarin glinting with gold in the sunlight, the Tarf with their striped bellies and four-handed swords, the tribesmen in their leather cloaks, the villagers with crude weapons and faces full of hate.

They stared, startled and agape, until they realized how small a troop it was and who was leading it.

A single voice, a woman's voice, cried out, "The Dark Man and the whore of Irnan!"

Mob shout, mob yell.

"The Dark Man and the whore!"

A woman, slim and naked, with body-paint laid on in whorls of pink and silver, pushed her way from the crowd and leaped onto a farm wagon abandoned in the fields. She was graceful and young and her hair was like a dark cloud around her head.

Stark knew her. "Baya."

So did Halk. "I told you then to kill her, Dark Man. Did I not?"

Baya shouted to the mob. "I was at Irnan! I saw the arrows fly. I saw the Wandsmen butchered. I saw the Farers slain . . . *because of them!*"

She flung out her arm toward Stark and Gerrith, her body bent like a bow.

"The star-spawn and the red-haired bitch whose mother made the prophecy!"

The mob gave tongue, a strange wild high-pitched scream.

Gerrith said, "That is the girl you brought from Skeg?"

"It is." Baya had made the first contact there with Stark, leading him to Gelmar and a deadly trap beside the milky sea. She had led the search for him after he escaped, when Yarrod and his group from Irnan hid him among the ruins beyond the river. Stark remembered how he had broken up a particularly nasty business involving two of Baya's Farer companions, high on love-weed, and had then been faced with the choice of killing the girl to keep her mouth shut or bringing her along on the journey to Irnan. He had chosen to do the latter. Mordach, Chief Wandsman of Irnan, freed her when he took Stark and Yarrod's people prisoner. Stark had not seen her again. He had wondered if she survived the slaughter in the city. Now he knew.

"These are the ones we came to take!" she was crying. "Let the traitors of Tregad rot behind their walls, we don't need them. Kill the Dark Man! Kill the whore! Kill! Kill! Kill!"

She leapt from the wagon and began to run across the turf, naked and lithe and light, hair flying behind her. Her name meant Graceful, and she was. Gerd snarled and lifted his hackles, his head against Stark's knee.

N'Chaka. Kill?

The blood-cry of the mob shook the heart. The Farers began to move, not as one man, but in groups, patches, swirls, until the whole of the mass was in motion. They were armed only with such things as stones and sticks and knives, an assortment of weapons as haphazard as themselves. But they were a good four thousand strong. They were not afraid.

The Fallarin had formed their crescent. They began to chant.

The tribesmen had swung into a V formation, with Stark and Halk at the apex and the villagers between the wings.

"Archers," said Stark. "And keep together. Head straight for the gate. Above all, don't stop."

Arrows were nocked to strings. The mob streamed toward them, a flapping bobbing grotesque multitude with that single slender form fleeting ahead.

The first sharp gust of wind knocked Baya from her feet. Her pink-and-silver body rolled on the green turf. The Fallarin moved forward, hunched in their saddles, dark wings beating, voices harsh and commanding. Magic or mind-force, the winds obeyed it. They whirled and beat, lashing hair and garments, pelting the Farers with leaves and twigs and heads of broken grain, chaff to sting and blind the eyes.

The mob mass faltered and began to stumble. The

123

winds drove group against group, spreading confusion which fed upon itself.

Stark raised his arm, and a tribesman in Hann purple put a horn to his lips and blew a strident call.

Stark said to the hounds, *Now kill!*

He kicked his beast into a run, heard the troop move behind him. Gerd ran at his knee. The winds dropped as suddenly as they had begun. Bowstrings twanged. He saw Farers dropping, spinning away. The floundering mob was split before him and he crashed on into the opening.

Fallarin and Tarf closed up swiftly behind the wings of the V. The beasts began to stumble over bodies. Halk was shouting a battle-cry that Stark had heard once before, in the square at Irnan: "Yarrod! Yarrod! Yarrod!" Stark looked at the gates of Tregad, and they were still far away and they were still shut. The mass of Farers seemed to be clotting and compacting ahead, between him and the gate.

There were too many of them. Swords rose and fell with increasing desperation. The hounds could not kill enough, could not kill fast enough. From out the milling screaming horde stones came flying. Stones are clodish weapons, without grace or beauty, but they function. Stark shouted, urging the men on, fighting off a horrible vision of the mob rolling in like water in the wake of the troop and submerging it by sheer weight of numbers.

Ponderously, with what seemed like dreamlike slowness, the gates of Tregad swung open.

Armed men poured out. A torrent of them. Hundreds of them. No sortie, but a full-scale attack. They fell upon the Farers with the ferocity of a long hatred, spilling blood into the fields as payment for the murdered grain.

Archers and slingers appeared upon the walls. A mounted troop rode out. Farers began to run. The solid mass broke. Bits of it shredded away, and the armed men moved through the chaos, smiting, until the shredding became a rout and the Farers were fleeing for the hills, leaving their dead in heaps amid the wreckage they had made.

A comparative quiet came over the field. Tregadians went among the wounded or leaned on their arms and stared at the strangers. Stark rallied his folk. Some had been hurt by flying stones, and one of the Tarf was dead. Three of the villagers were missing. He sent Sabak and some others to search for them.

Alderyk looked after the Farers, who were still being harried by the mounted troop and the more energetic foot. "The cold north has something to recommend it, after all," he said.

"You have the Runners."

"They don't pretend to be human," Alderyk said, "and we're not obliged to keep them fed."

The mounted troop turned and came back, having seen the Farers well on their way. An old man rode at the head of it, a fierce old man, all eyebrows and cheekbones and jut nose and thrusting chin. Locks of gray hair hung from under a round hard leather cap. His body-leather was worn and stained with use, and his sword was plain, with a broad blade and a sturdy grip, made for a day's work.

His black eyes probed at Stark, darted to Gerrith and Ashton, to the Fallarin and the Tarf, back to the hounds and Tuchvar. Those eyes were startlingly young and bright with angry excitement.

"You bring an interesting assortment of talents, Dark Man."

"Is that why you waited so long?" Stark asked. "To see what we could do?"

"I was impressed. Besides, it was my attack you were interfering with. I might ask you why you didn't wait until we were ready." He sheathed his sword. "I am Delvor, Warlord of Tregad." He bowed with a stiff courtliness to Alderyk and his Fallarin. "My lords, you are welcome in my city." In turn he greeted the others. "You find us at a moment of sudden event. Those ornaments on the wall are still warm."

He faced Stark abruptly and said, "Dark Man. I have heard one story and another story, all from Wandsmen

125

and Farers. Now I want to hear the true one. Has the Citadel fallen?"

"It has. Ask Ashton, who was prisoned there. Ask the Northhounds, who were its guardians. Ask the Hooded Men, who heard of it through Gelmar himself, the Chief Wandsman of Skeg."

Delvor nodded slowly. "I was sure, even though the Wandsmen said no and the Farers said lie. But it is strange, then . . ."

"What is?"

"The Lords Protector. The mighty ones who dwelt at the Citadel. Where are they? Or were they only a myth?"

"They're no myth," Stark said. "They're old men, red Wandsmen moved up to the top of the ladder where there's only room for seven. They wear white robes and do the ultimate thinking, remote and cool and unhurried by the urgencies of the moment. They make the policies that run your world, but they're making them at Ged Darod now, instead of at the Citadel."

"At Ged Darod," Delvor said. "The Lords Protector, undying and unchanging . . . Seven old men, turned out of their beds and their immortality, running for shelter at Ged Darod. Is this what you're telling me?"

"Yes."

"And yet there is no word of it? No beating of the breast, no crying of woe among the faithful? Those several thousand vermin didn't know it."

"They'll have to know in time," Stark said. "The Wandsmen can't keep it secret forever."

"No," said Halk. "But they haven't got to tell the truth, either." He looked almost himself again, holding the bloody sword, his face streaked with the sweat of battle. He laughed at Stark. "These Lords Protector are going to be harder to destroy than you thought, Dark Man."

"Come," said Delvor. "I forget my manners."

They rode toward the gate, and the soldiers of Tregad raised a ragged cheer.

Stark squinted up at the Wandsmen dangling on

126

the wall. "The red one wouldn't be Gelmar, I suppose?"

"No, that was our Chief Wandsman. One Welnic. Not a bad sort until he bethought him of his duty."

"What happened here?"

Delvor bent his black gaze upon the Farer dead sprawled amid crushed grain. "They came swarming out of the hills this morning. We're used to Farers, the gods know, but they run in small packs normally, drifting in and out. These were in their thousands, and for a purpose. We didn't like the look of them. We shut the gates. One of those—" He pointed to a green Wandsmen swinging gently in the breeze, "a one-eyed man, slightly mad, I think, was leading them. He raged at us, and Welnic insisted that he be let in to talk. So we let him through the postern, with the mob howling outside. They'd been sent from Ged Darod. It was thought that you were coming here to try and raise troops for Irnan, and they meant to trap you here in my city. I might not have minded that so much, since no decision had been made . . ."

"You were still waiting," Halk said, "for word from the north."

"Prophecies are all very well," said Delvor coldly, "but one does not go to war on the strength of a simple statement that thus or such will happen."

"We did."

"It was your prophecy. We preferred to wait." He gestured impatiently and got back to the subject. "The Farers had been brought to take over our city, to make sure that you got no help from us. The people of Tregad were to be used as hostages. They felt that you would hesitate to use your several weapons against us, and so you could be more easily disarmed and taken. We refused to have our people so endangered. That madman, that one-eyed swine, told us that if some of them had to die, it was in a good cause, and he bade us open the gate to his mob, which was already screaming threats and damaging our fields. We became even more angry when Welnic told us we would have to obey. When we did not, the

127

Wandsmen tried to open the gates themselves. You see where they ended."

His restless gaze stabbed at them. "They pushed us too far, you see. We might never have gone over. We might have sat debating and havering until Old Sun fell out of the sky. But they pushed us too far."

"So they did at Irnan," said Stark.

As they came under the wall, he was able to distinguish the individual features of the Wandsmen. Distorted and discolored as it was, there was no mistaking one of those faces, with the livid scar marring all of one side from brow to chin.

"Vasth," he said.

Halk, recognizing his handiwork, said harshly, "He will trouble decent men no more. You've done well here, Delvor."

"I hope so. There are many who will not agree."

"One thing puzzles me. Were there no mercenaries quartered on you, as there were at Irnan?"

"Only a token force. The rest had been sent as reinforcements to the siege. The Wandsmen were desperately anxious that Irnan should fall. I keep my men well trained to arms. We were able to deal with the mercenaries."

They passed in through the long tunnel of the gateway, into the square beyond, a cobbled space surrounded by walls of honey-colored stone. People straggled about, looking dazed by the swift turn of things, talking in low voices. They fell silent as the cavalcade came in and turned to stare. At the Dark Man and the whore of Irnan, Stark thought, wondering if Baya had escaped a second time.

Trail-worn and tired, they dismounted from their lean and footsore beasts; the tall desert beasts so out of place here. The tribesmen shook the dust from their cloaks and stood proudly, their veiled faces giving an impression of remote impassivity beneath their hoods, fierce eyes fixed resolutely on nothing, refusing to be awed by crowds or buildings.

The Fallarin, dainty as winged cats, stepped lightly

128

down. The hundred Tarf, in quiet ranks, blinked in mild unconcern at the townsfolk.

"I wonder," said Ashton, "that Gelmar didn't come himself to Tregad."

"Probably," Stark said, "he has something more important to attend to." His face hardened. "We all know that as soon as word of this day's work gets back to Ged Darod, Gelmar will be on his way to Skeg to shut down the starport."

20

It was warm in the woods, shadowed and warm and quiet. Branches were thick overhead, screening out Old Sun. The hollow was rimmed with flowering bushes and lined with golden moss. The tiny stream that ran through the hollow whispered and chuckled to itself, almost too softly to be heard. The smells were sweet and drowsy. Now and then a bird called somewhere, or some small creature rustled, or the brown shag-coated riding animals whuffled contentedly at their tethers. It was altogether a pleasant place to sit on an afternoon, after all the cold deserts and bitter winds and hard riding. Tuchvar had difficulty keeping his eyes open.

He had to. He was on watch.

Because he knew the way to Ged Darod and could handle the hounds, the Dark Man had chosen him as guide and companion. Him alone.

The hounds slept, thirteen great white sprawls on the moss. It saddened Tuchvar to see them so gaunt, and he tried to convince himself that they looked better than they had. They twitched and groaned and muttered in their sleep. He was aware of them as they dreamed; fleeting scraps of memory, of hunts and fights and mating and feeding and killing. The old hounds remembered mist and snow and the free-running of the pack.

The Dark Man slept, too, with Gerd's head resting on his thigh and Grith snoring by his other side. Tuchvar peeped at him sidelong, feeling like an intruder and afraid that at any moment those strange clear eyes would open and catch him at it. Even in sleep the man was powerful. Tuchvar felt that if he were to creep toward that muscled body, relaxed and sprawled like those of the hounds, no matter how quietly he went it would spring up all in a second before he could reach it, and those long-fingered hands would have him by the throat.

But they would not kill him until the brain behind the disconcerting eyes had considered and made that decision.

Control. That was the strength one felt in the Dark Man. Strength that went beyond the physical. Strength that the big tall man with the big long sword did not have, and perhaps that was why he disliked the Dark Man so much, because he knew that he lacked this strength himself, and envied it.

Stark's face fascinated Tuchvar. Had, since he first saw it there at Yurunna. He thought it was beautiful in its own way. Subtly alien. Brooding, black-browned, with a structure that might have been hammered out of old iron. A warrior's face, scarred by old battles. A killer's face, but without cruelty, and when he smiled it was like sunlight breaking through clouds. Now, in the unguarded innocence of sleep, Tuchvar saw something there that he had never noticed before. It was sadness. In his dreams, it seemed, the Dark Man remembered lost things and mourned them, not unlike the hounds.

He wondered where, across the wide and starry universe, on what remote and unimagined worlds, Stark might have lost those things, and what they might have been.

He wondered if he himself would ever get beyond the narrow skies of Skaith.

Not if the Wandsmen had their way.

It made him hurt inside to think that with one single word they could make those skies a prison for him, forever.

The Dark Man stirred, and Tuchvar became busy with the fastenings of his blue smock. He had put off the gray tunic of an apprentice Wandsman at Tregad. He had not chosen to wear it in the first place, and he had grown to hate it.

Being an ophan, he had come into the care of the Wandsmen; and Welnic, finding him more intelligent than most, had sent him to Ged Darod to be educated. That was a prideful thing, to be chosen, and even though he was made to study hard and learn the virtues of service and self-abnegation, the off-times in the lower city were a carnival, a fair that never ended.

Then they sent him north to Yurunna, and that was a different story. Cold and bleak, half-lifeless above the unpleasant oasis, the city had oppressed him with a sense of the unnatural. There was no laughter in those cheerless streets, no activity except the Yur, with their blank faces and empty eyes, going about their regimented business. One never saw their women or their young ones. No children played. No one ever sang, or shouted, or quarreled, or made music. There was nothing to do. The senior Wandsmen kept to themselves. The Houndmaster had been a harsh disciplinarian; Tuchvar had wept no tears for him, though he recognized the man's devotion to the hounds. He himself had become attached to the brutes for lack of anything better. Varik had not been much, as an only companion. He had elected with snuffling loyalty to remain with the Wandsman being held at Yurunna, rather than aid the forces of subversion. Tuchvar wondered how he was, and hoped that he was miserable.

It was Pedrallon and the Wandsmen's treatment of him that had made Tuchvar begin to question the system to which he was apprenticed.

His eyes were on the stars. He lived for the day when he could go to Skeg and actually see the ships and the men from other worlds. He was passionately on the side of the Irnanese, and he had worshipped Pedrallon, from his humble distance, for saying that the Irnanese were right and the Wandsmen wrong. And then Pedrallon had been silenced, punished, put to shame. He himself had been given a tongue-lashing by his mentor and soon after had found himself packed off to Yurunna.

He had begun to think, for the first time in his life. Really think, trying to separate the deed from the word and the word from the truth, getting hopelessly confused because here there was nothing one could put one's hand on, only uncertainties and perhapses. But he decided at the last that in any case he wanted the stars more than he wanted to be a Wandsman, and if the Wandsmen were going to forbid him the stars, he would fight them in any way he could.

Beyond the trees, shimmering in the midst of the plain, lay Ged Darod, golden roofs and thronging multitudes, with the great towers of the upper city reared like a benison over all. Memories swept across Tuchvar's mind in a crushing wave, memories of power, deep-seated and very old, as strong as the foundations of the world. His belly contracted with a pang of dismal certainty.

Surely not even the Dark Man could overcome that power.

He wanted to pound his fists against all frustration. Why were grown men so blind, so stupid, so stubborn, when the answers to everything were so clear and simple? He had stayed for hours in the state hall at Tregad, with its fine pillars and sturdy arches carved in patterns of vines and fruit, listening to the speeches and the arguments. Some were still concerned with the rightness or wrongness of what had been done, as though that mattered now. Some demanded that the city take the Dark Man and his companions prisoner and hand them over to the Wandsmen in the hope of buying forgiveness. These people had had to be forcibly silenced when the Dark Man and his people spoke, telling of the Citadel and Yurunna and urging

132

help for Irnan as a means of freeing Tregad from the yoke of the Wandsmen.

And of course that was the thing to do. Tuchvar could not understand why there was any question about it, why they did not at once raise every man they could spare and march to Irnan. Yet still they talked and argued.

Some said they ought to shut themselves up behind their walls and wait to see what happened. Others wrangled about the starships—whether or not they were worth fighting for, whether or not some or all of the people should emigrate, whether or not both those questions were fruitless because in any case the Wandsmen would send the ships away. Men and women yelled and screamed at each other. Finally Delvor had risen, in his iron and worn leather, and fixed them his fierce glare.

"The stars are nothing to me one way or the other," he said. "Skaith was my mother, and I'm over old for fostering. But I tell you this: Whatever you want, life on another world or a better life right here, you will have to fight for it, and not with words or halfhearts, and you cannot fight alone. The first blow has been struck. Let us strike the second. Let us march to relieve Irnan. And let word be sent among all the city-states that the Citadel has fallen, that the Lords Protector are human and vulnerable men, that we fight for our own freedom, and if they want to get the bloody Farers off their backs, they had better damned well join us!"

Someone had yelled, "Tell 'em to try hanging up a few Wandsmen! It's tonic for the soul."

There had been a lot of cheering, and the majority of people in the hall, those who had had little to say, began to shout, "On to Irnan!" Then somebody shouted, "Yarrod! Yarrod!" like a battle cry, and so the decision was finally made in a bedlam of noise, and Tuchvar understood dimly that this had been the only possible decision all along and that the people had known it.

A little later he had asked the off-worlder with the

kind eyes, the man called Ashton for whom Stark had a special look, why it had taken them so long.

"The city-states are democracies," Ashton said. "The curse of all democracies is that they talk too much. On the other hand, the Wandsmen haven't got to talk at all. They simply decree."

So now men were marching toward Irnan, and that had pleased the tall warrior Halk.

The wise woman, with her thick bronze braid of hair and her splendid body, had not seemed happy at all when she said good-bye to Stark. Tuchvar thought he had seen tears glint at the corners of her eyes when she turned away.

He could not know it, but the Dark Man was reliving, in his dreams, an earlier moment spent with Gerrith, the two of them quite alone.

"I have seen a knife, Stark."

"You saw one before, remember? And it was good."

"This is not good."

"Where is the knife? Who wields it?"

"I cannot see . . ."

And her lips came against his, and he tasted salt upon them, the salt of tears . . .

Stark woke, and was in the hollow with Tuchvar and the hounds, and Ged Darod out on the plain. He wondered if the knife waited for him somewhere in those streets. Then he shrugged the thought aside. Knives were no new thing to him. Nor was being wary.

While the boy took food from the saddlebags, Stark went through the trees to where the wood ended above a cliff and he could look out over the plain, green and lush, with Ged Darod in the middle of it like a dream. Golden roofs, roofs tiled and lacquered in scarlet and green and cobalt blue, flashed and glittered in the sunlight. The upper city was built on a slight rise, natural or artificial, and the massive buildings there, with their soaring towers, were of a pure whiteness unrelieved by any color. Roads crossed the plain from all directions, converging upon the city, and the roads were thronged with pilgrims, indistinct masses of tiny figures moving in a haze of dust.

He went back to the hollow and said to Tuchvar, "Tell me again where I will find Pedrallon."

"If he's still kept there . . ."

"I understand that. Tell me."

Tuchvar told him, while he ate and drank, and washed in the running stream, and the sunlight slanted lower. Then the boy watched while Stark opened a bundle and took out the things he had brought from Tregad. Tuchvar had a special interest because Stark had consulted with him on what habit might pass without notice among the mass of pilgrims.

A cloak to conceal somewhat his height and his manner of walking. A hood to cover his head, and a mask or veil, after the manner of the Hooded Men, to hide his face. Stark had considered borrowing a cloak from one of his troopers. He decided against it; any member of any one of the Seven Hearths of Kheb would be a matter of interest to the Wandsmen on sight, and the Farers who had seen the troop at Tregad would pose too much of a threat. So he had chosen a cloak of coarse gray homespun, with a deep hood of a different cut and a cloth of faded blue to wrap about his face. Tuchvar had seen pilgrims in every sort of garb; and some hid this, and some that, and some nothing; he thought Stark's choice of garments would not draw notice.

But when Stark turned to him and asked, "Will I pass," Tuchvar sighed and shook his head.

"You are too much you," he said. "Let your shoulders hang, and don't look at anyone straight . . . you have not a pilgrim's eyes."

Stark smiled. He spoke to the hounds, ordering them to stay with the boy and wait for his return. The young hounds were not concerned. The five whined, Gerd and Grith protesting. In the end they obeyed, though not happily.

Guard Tuchvar, Stark said, *until I come.* He went away between the trees, in the deepening dusk.

21

By the time Stark reached the nearest road, far out across the green plain, it was full night. The Three Ladies rode the sky, serene and splendid, shedding a sweeter light than that of Old Sun, a light almost as bright. He was able to see that the number of pilgrims had not diminished. Half of Skaith, it seemed, was on the way to Ged Darod.

He moved through a thin scatter of stragglers dropped out beside the road and slipped into the stream.

His nose twitched, under the veil, to a variety of smells. Warm dust. Bodies washed and scented, bodies unwashed and stinking. Beast-flesh, sweaty, pungent. An underlying heavy sweetness of potent substances smoked or chewed.

The stream was irregular, moving at different speeds within itself. It clotted up around a huge teetering construction like a wheeled temple, drawn and pushed by scores of naked men and women painted the holy brown of Skaith-Mother. It thinned again to a mere trickle of slow-footed walkers. Everyone moved at his own speed. Close to Stark, completely preoccupied, a man in a dirty shift was dancing his way to Ged Darod, three steps forward, leap, whirl, stamp, then three more steps and whirl again. Beyond him, a woman with hair hanging to her heels, all twined with flowers, moved like a somnambulist, arms held stiffly in front of her; she sang as she went in a high clear voice as sweet as a lark's.

A lank holy man, tattooed from crown to foot with sun symbols, cried out ecstatically to Stark, "Rejoice, for we shall be cleansed of evil!"

Stark muttered, "I rejoice," and passed him by, wondering.

There were others in the stream wearing hooded cloaks, others with their faces hidden. No one gave Stark any special notice. Remembering Tuchvar's caution, he tried not to stride too fast, with too much purpose—a purpose which, he knew all too well, might be completely futile.

It was only a guess, based on the incoherent sobbings of a terrified man, that Pedrallon and his people had ever had a transceiver, let along that they still had it and were in a position to use it. Pedrallon himself might now be dead or incarcerated too deeply for anyone to find. He might have repented his sins and put himself back in the good graces of the Twelve, in which case even to ask about him would be dangerous. Simply entering Ged Darod was a gigantic risk.

Yet it had to be taken. Otherwise he and Simon Ashton could resign themselves to living out such lives as might be left to them on Mother Skaith, and the Irnanese could forget about emigrating. Short of a miracle. True, shutting down the starport and banishing the ships might lead to scattered landings by avaricious star-captains looking for gain. Some of them, or one of them, might land near Irnan or Tregad and might even accept passengers. But it was too much of a gamble to be taken if there was even a slight chance of communicating with Skeg in time.

Tuchvar had told him that the number of folk on the road was not unusual for this season of the year, and perhaps that was so. Yet Stark felt a strange mood among them. Anticipation. The excitement of great events occurring or about to occur; the excitement of being a part of them. He had no idea if some specific word had been spread among them or if he was witnessing one of those mystic hysterias that sweep over the less stable elements of a population from time to time like an air borne plague. Whichever it was, there were curious echoes in the cries he heard.

From a kind of bower at the top of the great creaking temple thing, a priestess, done up with artificial at-

137

tributes that would have shocked Skaith-Daughter, kept shouting at the night that all blasphemies would be expunged and all blasphemers punished. A carriage of gilded wood went by, carrying a party of folk from the tropic south, slender men and women in bright silks, their rapt small faces cameos cut in amber. They too cried out about punishments and the feeding of Old Sun. Stark went on, and the distant roofs of Ged Darod glistened ahead, in the light of the Three Ladies.

It was strange that there were no folk going the other way, no pilgrims leaving the city.

He passed a group of men all in yellow robes. Podmasters, seeking more sanctity before they took on another mindless and happy group to lead to communal oblivion and the ultimate fulfillment, death.

He passed more dancers, three women this time, holding hands. Their hair covered their faces. Their white limbs gleamed through flowing garments. There was music for them to dance to, a plucking and twangling of strings, a swelling and fading of pipes, where here and there a pilgrim beguiled his way. But the women did not hear that music. They were listening to a secret melody of their own, measured and solemn.

A large band of Farers grabbed at Stark's cloak and cried, "Words, pilgrim! We will hear words tonight. Are you ready for the truth?" Their eyes were glassy, their breathing heavy with sweet drugs. "The truth that casts out lies and castrates evil?"

"I am ready," Stark answered in a voice of thunder. "Are you? Embrace each other! Love!"

They laughed and did as he told them. One of the women flung her arms about him and kissed him, her lips hot through the veil.

"Stay a while, at the side of the road. I'll show you love." She nuzzled at the veil, catching at it with her teeth. "Why do you hide yourself?"

"I've taken a vow," said Stark, and thrust her gently away.

There was a clear space on the road, where only one

138

man walked alone, eyes fixed on the white towers of Ged Darod.

"They succor the weak, they feed the hungry, they shelter the homeless. They are our fathers, the Lords Protector. They give us all we need."

The man repeated this like a litany. Stark looked into his face and knew that he was on his way to die.

Behind him along the road he began to hear a disturbance. He turned. A party of mounted men moved toward him at a businesslike pace, threading their way through the people, sometimes getting off the road entirely to bypass an obstacle. They were not pilgrims.

Stark melted into the nearest group, which drew aside to make room. The hard-ridden beasts came shouldering by, with six riders. Four of them were Wandsmen. The other two were wrapped and hooded in black cloaks.

Glancing up from under his own hood, Stark caught a glimpse of a face, furred, snow-white, with the great shining eyes of a creature who dwells away from the sun.

For a fleeting second he thought those eyes met his, in the gentle light of the Three Ladies.

A stab of alarm shot through him. But the riders went on; there was no outcry, and if the person in the black cloak had indeed noticed him, there had been no recognition. Stark pulled his veil higher and his hood lower and continued on, not happy with what he had seen.

These were Children of Skaith-Our-Mother. Kell à Marg's folk from the catacombs under the Witchfires. He even thought that he knew the one and could make a guess at the other. Fenn and Ferdic, who had come at him with daggers in the Hall of the Diviners.

He didn't know what they were doing at Ged Darod, so far to the south, out in the open world under the sky they had forsaken so long ago. He did know that he had enough enemies already in the city. He did not need any more.

The walls of Ged Darod rose out of the plain, and there was light above them like a glowing dome. The gates stood open, always open. There were a dozen gates, and each gate served a road. The streams of pilgrims poured through them into the City of the Wandsmen.

It was a city of sound as well as light, and the sound was bells. They hung from the edges of the tiered roofs. They climbed the spires and girdled the golden domes. Thousands of them, swinging free to greet with their clapper tongues each passing breeze, so that the air was full of a sweet soft chiming.

Down in the streets was a fragrance of incense and a jostling of crowds that seemed to lack all rancor, in spite of the numbers of pilgrims that continued to be absorbed into them. People squatted or lay against the walls of the buildings. Balconies overhead held more. Runnels of water went everywhere in stone channels, by way of sanitation, and there was a reason for the incense. It was impossible to provide accommodation for everyone, and the Farers preferred the streets in any case.

Stark was only interested in one hostel, and that was the Refuge, where the Farer girls went to have their babes and leave them for the Wandsmen to rear.

He took his bearings, by Tuchvar's instructions, on a scarlet roof with ten tiers and plunged into the teeming streets.

22

As he walked, he became increasingly aware of the mood of the city.

It waited. It waited with held breath. It waited, like a nerve stretched and rasped beyond endurance, for relief. Each fresh incursion of pilgrims seemed to heighten and exacerbate the tension. The city was a catchbasin, filled to overflowing, with everything coming in and nothing going out.

Yet the people were aimless. They wandered through the streets, thronged into the temples, spilled into squares and gardens. They danced and sang and made love. They prayed and chanted. There were many hostels and places where food and drink were dispensed at all hours. The Wandsmen provided everything their children desired, and Wandsmen of the lesser ranks moved about the city seeing that all was in order.

In the quiet enclaves of Ged Darod, between the temple complex and the upper city, were hospitals for the sick and aged, creches for the orphaned and unwanted, homes for the disabled. No one was turned away, though most of the adult inmates were Farers gone in years who had long ago abandoned home and family and so had nowhere else to go when their Faring days were over.

The temples were magnificent. The ones with the golden roofs were sacred to Old Sun. The others, no less beautiful, belonged to Skaith-Mother, Sea-Mother, Sky-Father and several aspects of the Dark Goddess of the high north and antarctic south. Pilgrims eddied slowly through these vast and solemn spaces, staring at richnesses and beauties such as they had never seen. Awed into silence, they made their offerings and did their worship and went away feeling that they had helped their world to live a little bit longer. The true ecstatics remained until they were gently carried away by the temple custodians.

These were the great temples, the powerful deities. There was a multitude of smaller ones. Even Tuchvar could not say who and what all these deities were or how they were worshipped. There were tales told in the apprentice dormitories at night that might or might not be true. Stark doubted nothing. On Skaith, anything at all was possible.

He came to the Great House of Old Sun, the largest of all the temples, a stunning splendor with its golden roofs and white pillars, all reflected in the huge tank that fronted it. A wall surrounded the tank, a stony lacework of tiny niches, and in each niche a candle burned, so that the water gleamed with a million tiny points of fire. People were bathing in the holy water, in the holy candlefire that symbolized the light of Old Sun, who drives away death and darkness.

Stark went along the right-hand side of the tank, past the temple, and into a street where souvenir sellers offered sun symbols in every size and substance. At the end of this street, Tuchvar had told him, he would see the walls surrounding the Refuge.

Purest white in the light of the Three Ladies, the buildings of the upper city stood above the jumbled roofs like a cliff. Rows and rows of small windows, identical in size, betokened the myriad chambers that lay behind that pale facade. There was much more hidden behind it: a vast complex of living quarters, schools, seminaries and administrative offices, forbidden to the public. Crowning it all was the palace of the Twelve, second only to the Citadel in its importance to the Wandsmen.

The street was clogged, like all the others, with far too many people. Stark moved snail-like, not daring to push and shove, keeping his head down whenever one of the Wandsmen appeared. He strained for a sight of the Refuge, hoping that some way would be apparent for him to approach the building without attracting attention.

He never saw it.

A deep-toned bell pealed out from somewhere high up in the white towers. The sweet chiming of the smaller bells was drowned instantly in that mighty tolling, the prattle of cherubs overborne by the voice of God.

It was the summons for which the city had been waiting, and all over Ged Darod people roused from their aimlessness and began to move.

Trapped in that irresistible tide, Stark moved with them.

He was carried by side streets away from the Refuge, into a vast square below the Wandsmen's city, where an arched gateway pierced the white and many-windowed cliff. The gateway was a tunnel, stepped, rising out of sight. At the nearer end above the square there was a platform thrusting out, a kind of stage.

The bell boomed out its call over the shining roofs, steady, mesmeric, echoed in throbbing eardrums and the beating of the blood. The faithful poured into the square until it could hold no more, and the surrounding streets were blocked by solid masses of humanity. Stuck fast, Stark could do no more than try to work his way by slow degrees toward a place at the edge of the square where there were no buildings. The press was so great that he could not see what was hemming in the crowd there. Whatever it might be, that was the direction in which he wanted to go, for it offered the only hope of openness and possible escape from this heaving, breathing, muttering, stinking trap of bodies.

The bell fell silent.

For a moment the sound continued in Stark's ears—then stillness again, and gradually the sweet small tinkling that seemed very far away now, a mere backdrop for the silence.

A company of Wandsmen in blue tunics came down the steps of the gate, bearing torches. They set the torches in standards around the platform. They drew back and waited.

A company of Wandsmen dressed in green paced down the steps and took up places.

A wait, interminable, bringing a whimper as of pain from the crowd.

The red Wandsmen came, a moving patch of dark crimson in the torchlight. They came in procession, four by four, down the steps and onto the platform, some before and some behind; and in their midst were the Lords Protector, spotless white.

A gasp of indrawn breath from the crowd as the seven men in their white robes moved forward, and then the puzzled whispers began, tossing like surf across the square.

"Who are they? What Wandsmen wear white?"

And of course, Stark thought, they didn't know.

They couldn't know. Never in the world before this minute had they seen a Lord Protector.

He began to have a cold premonition of what was coming.

A red Wandsman stepped to the front of the platform and lifted his wand of office like a baton.

"My children!"

His harsh and sonorous voice carried clearly for an amazing distance, and when it reached its limits, other voices took up the message and passed it back through the far ranks of the crowd.

"My children, this is a night of great tidings. A night of joy, a night of hope. The messengers of the Lords Protector have come out of the high north to speak to you. Be silent, then, and listen!"

He stepped, giving place to one of the white robes.

Ferdias. Even at that distance there was no mistaking the ramrod stance and the noble head.

The crowd snuffled and panted in its intense effort to be absolutely still.

"My children," said Ferdias, and his voice was a benison, an outpouring of love. "This has been a time of trial. You have heard many things that were difficult to understand—prophecies of doom, news of revolt and disobedience and the slaying of Wandsmen . . ."

The crowd growled like a monstrous beast.

"Now you will hear more tales. Men will tell you that the prophecy of Irnan was a true prophecy, that the Citadel has fallen to the despoiling hands of a stranger and that the Lords Protector themselves are brought down."

Ferdias waited out the response, holding up his hands.

"It is not true, my children! The Citadel has not fallen, cannot fall. The Citadel is not stone and timber to be burned by a careless torch. It is faith and love, a thing of the spirit, beyond the touch of any man. The Lords Protector who dwell there, undying, unchanging, forever watchful over your needs, are beyond the power of any man to harm. We, their humble servants, who are privileged to hear their wishes, are sent now to bid you forget these lies, to let you know that you are, as always, safe in their protecting care."

Under cover of the tumult, Stark managed to worm his way closer to the edge of the crowd, yelling joyfully with the rest, a sick anger gnawing at his belly. So much for his vaunted destruction of the Lords Protector. There had been an excellent reason for keeping the Citadel so remote; he remembered Skaith-Daughter's cynical remark that invisibility was a condition of godhead. Try now to tell this screaming rabble who the seven old men in white really were!

Ferdias was speaking again, his calm strong voice ringing out; father-voice, firm and kind and true.

"All the evil and disruption that beset us stem from one single event—the coming of the starships. The Lords Protector have been patient because of the benefits these ships could bring to you, their children. And because they love all men, they hoped that the aliens, the strange men from worlds beyond our knowledge, might understand and share that love."

The voice suddenly became a whipcrack.

"It was not so. The strange men brought poison. They encouraged our people to rebel. They threatened our faith. They struck at the very foundations of our society. Now the Lords Protector have made their decision. The ships must go from Skaith, they must be forever gone!"

A subtle change in Ferdias' voice, and Stark had the queer feeling that the Lord Protector was speaking directly to him.

"This night the starport will be closed. There will be no more talk of emigration." The voice paused; barbed and toothed, it spoke again. "There will be no more escape."

Raving and yelling like the idiots around him, Stark moved a little farther and saw a stone balustrade at the edge of the crowd. Beyond it were the tops of trees. Farther beyond, somewhere out of sight, were the walls of the Refuge.

And at Skeg, where the starships stood like towers

145

beside the sea, Gelmar would be marshaling his forces.

The red Wandsman had come again to the fore, waving his arms and his wand, signing the crowd to be quiet.

"Be still and listen! There is more. We have reason to believe that the Dark Man himself, the evil man of the prophecy, may be here in Ged Darod, may be among us now. If so, he wears a hooded cloak and all but his eyes are hidden. You will know him by—"

Stark did not wait to hear what they would know him by, if they took the time to look. He charged like a bull for the balustrade and went over it.

The bastard son of Skaith-Our-Mother had noticed him after all.

23

Tree branches broke his fall. Turf soft and springy as a mattress received him twenty feet below. Stark hit rolling and was on his feet and running before the first man after him came down, too swiftly for his own good, and lay screaming over a broken leg.

Thrashings in the trees told of others climbing down more cautiously. Bedlam had broken out in the square above. Only a small number of people would have seen Stark's leap over the balustrade, and even they could not be certain of his identity. Every man in Ged Darod who had chosen to wear a hooded cloak would at that moment be fighting for his life or running for it as Stark was.

Stark kept his own cloak on until he was out of sight of the people above. No point in letting them see him without it. A small private arbor of vines drooping great pendant flowers gave shelter. He stripped off the cloak and mask and thrust them in among rugs and cushions that rather surprisingly covered the floor. Then he ran again, cursing the name of Fenn, or Ferdic, whichever it might be.

That fleeting instant on the road in which their eyes had met must have remained in the creature's consciousness, pricking at him until he noticed it and began to wonder. Then he began to picture to himself the Earthman's appearance, in the Hall of the Diviners, where they had tried to kill him, and before, in Kell à Marg's throne-room, and he began to think, "Yes, those eyes, the very look and color, and I could swear they knew me."

Damn the Three beautiful Ladies. Damn the night-seeing eyes of a burrowing animal.

Not sure. He could not have been sure. But what did he, or the Wandsmen, have to lose by trying? Only the lives of a few pilgrims who would die at the hands of the mob. A small sacrifice for the chance of catching the Dark Man.

Beyond the arbors were more arbors, amid fountains throwing sprays of scented water. There were broad swards set with curious statuary and peculiar apparatus. There were pavilions with curtains of scarlet silk. There were mazes set with little secret bowers. There were silvery pools that promised delight, and gossamer cages swung high from gaily painted poles to dip and bob in the air. Stark knew where he was now. These were the Pleasure Gardens of Ged Darod, and if it had not been for the summons of the bell, the gardens would have been busy with folk playing at various games, in groups and couples.

There was little pleasure here for Stark. He dodged and darted, using every bit of cover. He outdistanced his pursuers. But even though they had lost sight of him, they hung on, fanning out to search every shadow where he might be hiding, yelping at each other like curs on the track of a wolf.

Outside the gardens, Ged Darod would be in a ferment, with crowds rushing this way and that after victims, their blood-lust at fever pitch. Stark felt the living weight of the city all about him, a devouring entity from which he had little chance of escape.

He fled on in the direction of the Refuge, thinking grimly that he might as well. No place else offered any hope at all. If Pedrallon was by a miracle still there, Stark might be able through him to salvage something out of the ruin, in spite of Ferdias.

There was a sunken place within the garden, paved in patterns of lustrous tile depicting various symbols of Skaith-Mother in her aspect as a fertility goddess. Slim pillars of varying heights were set about, and atop each one was a perch where a creature rested and lazily fanned iridescent wings; huge jewel-colored things resembling butterflies, except that each body was luminous. They glowed like silver lamps upon their perches, and their wings fanned perfume.

"They are dazed with nectar," someone said. "Sodden with honey. Their dreams are sweet."

He saw the woman.

She stood beside a pillar, one arm outstretched to touch it. Her garment was mist-gray and it clung to her like mist, softly, with her full, rounded, graceful body glimmering through it. Her hair was black, coiled high and held by an oddly shaped coronet of hammered silver set with a green stone.

Her eyes were the color of a winter sea where the sun strikes it. He had never seen such eyes. They had depths and darknesses and tides of sudden light in which a man might lose himself and drown.

"I am Sanghalain of Iubar, in the White South," she said. She smiled. "I have waited for you."

"Not another seeress!" said Stark, and he smiled, too, though he could hear the yelping pack in the distance.

She shook her head, and then Stark saw another figure among the pillars.

"My comrade Morn," she said, "has the gift of mind-touch. It is the habit of his people, who live where other speech is difficult."

Morn came forward and stood behind the woman towering above her, huge-eyed and strange. Not human, Stark thought; not mutated by choice like the Children of the Sea. Some sort of amphibian mammal naturally evolved. He was hairless, with smooth-gleaming skin, dark on the back, light on the belly, camouflage against deep-swimming predators. The smooth skin oozed sweat, and the deep chest heaved uncomfortably. He wore a garment of leather, polished black and worked with gold lines, very rich in appearance, and he carried a trident, its long haft inlaid with gold wire and pearls.

"When we first learned that you might be in the city, we realized you must have come to find Pedrallon. Nothing else could have brought you here. So we stayed by the Refuge while Morn tried to find you. There are so many minds. Not until you broke away from the crowd was he able to recognize you and say where you were. Then we came to meet you." She reached out and took his hand. "We must hurry."

He went with Sanghalain of Iubar and round-eyed Morn, moving silently and at a pace that spoke of urgency. The yelping of the pack diminished as they left the Pleasure Gardens and went by narrow ways that brought them abruptly to a courtyard. Stark saw a coach and a baggage wagon, each with a human driver, and an escort of Morn's folk armed and waiting beside their mounts. The night had grown darker, with the setting of the first of the Three Ladies.

"We were on the point of leaving Ged Darod when the word was brought," said Sanghalain. "Quickly, Stark. Into the coach."

He halted. "No. I came to see Pedrallon."

"He's gone. When he learned that your forces had taken Yurunna, he found means to disappear."

"Where is he, then?"

"I don't know. I have been promised that I will be taken to him." An imperious note came into her voice; she was used to command and impatient of obstruction. "We've already risked a good deal to save you, Stark. Get in, unless you wish to die in this madhouse."

A mournful far-off something spoke in his mind like the distant crying of a seabird.

She speaks the truth. We wait no longer.

Morn shifted the heavy trident in his hands.

Stark hesitated only briefly. He got in.

The coach was a heavy thing constructed for long journeys rather than for grace of line. It was made of a black wood, carved and polished, and it had a hood of fine leather against sun and rain. Inside were soft rugs and cushions on a padded floor, so that a lady might ride in comfort, and at the rear was a compartment where things to be used at night or in cold weather could be stored out of the way.

The compartment had been emptied. At Sanghalain's direction Stark crammed himself into it, and she deftly covered him with spare rugs, arranged the cushions and leaned herself against them.

He could feel her weight. Almost before it was settled, the coach began to move. Hard hoofs drummed and clattered on the stones. There was the creak and jingle of harness and the clacking of the wheels. Other than that there was no sound. If Morn and his folk had speech at all, they did not use it.

The company left the courtyard and went a little way at a fair pace. Then the streets of Ged Darod closed around them.

Sounds echoed strangely in Stark's wooden box. Voices boomed and roared, sometimes indistinct, sometimes with startling clarity.

"Irnan! On to Irnan! Save the siege!"

And something was said about the Dark Man.

Fists pounded on the body of the coach. It rocked and jolted where the crowd pushed against it in spite of the mounted escort. Movement was slowed to a crawl. Still, they did move. They moved for a long time. Stark thought they must be nearing one of the gates. Then Sanghalain spoke sharply, just loud enough for him to hear.

"Be very quiet. Wandsmen."

The coach halted. Stark heard the same harsh sonorous voice that had spoken from the platform.

"You're in great haste to leave us, Lady Sanghalain."

Her answer was as cold as the waves that break along the foot of an iceberg.

"I came here to ask help. I did not receive it. I no longer have any reason to remain."

"Would it not have been wiser to wait for morning?"

"If you want the truth, Jal Bartha, I find your city disgusting and your rabble loathsome. I prefer to be away from both as soon as possible."

"You take a harsh attitude, my lady. It was explained to you why your request could not be granted. You must have faith in the Lords Protector. All will be made right in time."

"In time," said Sanghalain, "we shall all be dead and beyond caring. Be kind enough to stand aside, Jal Bartha."

The coach began faltering on its way again. After an interminable period the motion became freer. Noise and jostling subsided. The pace picked up.

Stark dared for the first time to move, easing cramped muscles.

Sanghalain said, "Not yet. Too many on the road." A little later she added, "It will soon be dark."

When the last of the Three Ladies had set, some time would elapse before Old Sun rose. Stark had no idea what direction they had taken from Ged Darod, nor who the Lady Sanghalain was, or where Iubar might be in the White South; and he could not be sure that she was telling the truth about Pedrallon, though it sounded reasonable. The one thing he was sure of was that she had saved his life, and he decided to be content with that. For the rest of it, he was forced to contain his soul and his aching bones in such patience as he could muster—thinking of the ships at Skeg, thinking of the flame and thunder of their going, thinking of himself and Ashton left behind.

The coach turned sharply off the road and went for a long distance over open ground. After a lot of jolting and bouncing it came to a halt and Sanghalain pulled away the cushions.

"It's safe now."

He climbed out as from a coffin, gratefully. It was dark. He made out branches against the sky and the trunks of trees against a lesser gloom beyond. They were in some kind of a grove. The escort had lighted down and were tending their beasts.

"Care was taken that no one should see us leave the road," said Sanghalain. "We are to wait here until the Wandsman comes."

24

Stark stared at the pale blur of her face in the gloom, wishing he could see her eyes, marking the place where her throat would be.

He said very softly, "What Wandsman?"

She laughed. "What menace! There is no danger, Dark Man. If I had wanted to betray you, I could have done it more easily at Ged Darod."

"What Wandsman?"

"His name is Llandric. It was he who told me about Pedrallon. Who told me that one of the strangers in the black cloaks thought he might have seen you on the road. Llandric is Pedrallon's man."

"Can you be so sure?"

"Very sure. No one lies to Morn."

"And Morn was present?"

"Morn is always present at such a time. I could not rule Iubar without Morn."

Again the far sad voice in Stark's mind, dim echoing of sea caves under storm.

She tells the truth. No treachery.

Stark let himself relax. "Does Pedrallon still have access to the transceiver?"

"So I was told. I understand it is a thing that speaks over distances almost as quickly as the Ssussminh do."

152

She gave the word a long rolling sound, *Soosmeeng,* like surf on shingle, and Stark understood that she referred to Morn's people.

"Where is it?"

"Wherever Pedrallon is. We must wait."

Wait and be patient, he thought, while Gelmar is sweeping Skeg clean with his broom of Farers.

The driver of the coach brought wine in a leather bottle and two silver cups. They drank, in the mild night, and Stark listened, hearing nothing but the rustle of leaves overhead, the cropping and stamping and blowing of the beasts.

"What brought you to Ged Darod?" he asked her. "What did you want from the Wandsmen that you didn't get?" Her attitude toward the red Wandsman Jal Bartha had indeed been harsh.

"The same thing the people of Irnan asked for and didn't get," she answered. "Our life has become all but intolerable."

"Because of the Wandsmen?"

"No. We're too far away for Farers and oppression, not rich enough to warrant mercenaries. So poor, in fact, and so unimportant that I thought they wouldn't stop our going. I came all this long way north, in the hope—"

She broke off. He sensed her anger, the same futile rage he himself had felt as he battered at the stone wall of the Wandsmen's power. He also sensed that there were no tears ready to come. Sanghalain was too strong for that.

"Where is Iubar?"

"Far to the south, where a peninsula juts into the Great Sea of Skaith. We used to be a prosperous country of fisherfolk and farmers and traders. Our galleys went everywhere, and if we had then to pay our tithes to the Wandsmen, we had enough. Things are different now. The great bergs come from the south, as do the blind mists, to kill our ships. Snow lies deep and long on our fields. The Children of the Sea despoil our fisheries, and the Kings of the White Isles raid our shores. I and my order have some power to protect, but we cannot heal Mother Skaith, who is dying. If we move north, we must fight for every foot of land against the folk who hold it, and they are stronger than we. Whichever way we look, we see death." She paused and added, "A madness has begun to creep among our people, which is even worse."

She was silent for a time. Stark, listening, heard nothing beyond the grove.

She was talking again, her voice low, with a hint of weariness. "Traders and sea gypsies brought us tales of the starships and the men from beyond the sky. We considered, and it seemed that here was a possibility of escape for our people. I took ship and came north to Skeg, to see for myself. The starships were there, and the foreign men, but I was not allowed to approach them. The Wandsmen would not permit it. When I asked them where I could obtain permission, they told me the authority was at Ged Darod. At Ged Darod I was told—but you know what they said, and so my long journey was for nothing, unless Pedrallon can help." She laughed with intense bitterness. "The strangers in the black cloaks had come to ask that the starships be sent away for the safety of Mother Skaith. But the Lords Protector had already taken that step, so they too had made their trip for nothing."

Morn's voice echoed in Stark's mind. *He comes. Alone.*

It was several minutes before Stark's ears picked up the soft thudding of hoofs. A man rode in among the trees, a dim shape, dark on a dark mount.

"Lady Sanghalain?" His voice was young, strained with excitement and an awareness of danger. It broke off, quivering, as he became aware of Stark's bulk beside the woman. "Who is that?"

"Eric John Stark," he said. "I am called the Dark Man."

Silence. Then a letting out of held breath. "You did escape. Ged Darod has been seething with rumors. Some said you were killed . . . I saw several bodies. Others said you were concealed somewhere, or had got away, or had never been there at all. Jal Bartha and

154

the Children of Skaith were all over the city looking at the dead—"

Stark cut him short. "We wish to see Pedrallon."

"Yes. My lady, we'll have to leave the coach and wagon here, and your escort, too."

"Not Morn."

"All right, but no more. Can you ride?"

"As well as you." She caught up a cloak, and Morn lifted her from the coach to the back of one of the beasts. "Give Stark one, too."

"How far have we to go?"

"An hour's hard ride to the east," said Llandric, sounding less than happy that his expected party of two had doubled. Probably he would have preferred to have Pedrallon's permission. If that gave him problems, Stark couldn't help it.

They came out of the grove into the open starlight of the plain; starlight dim enough to prevent them being seen at any great distance.

Even so, Llandric was nervous.

"The Farers are out," he said. "Wandsmen are leading them to the siege. Did Tregad send a force to Irnan?"

"It's on its way now."

"So is an army of Farers, with a short road through the mountains."

Several times they saw torches in the distance, tiny flecks of fire moving across the landscape. Stark hoped that Tuchvar and the hounds were safely hidden in the hollow. The lad would have to use his own judgment if things became threatening.

The country turned rougher and wilder, smooth plain giving way to tumbled hummocks and clumps of tough grass that made bad footing for the animals. Llandric urged them on, peering anxiously at the sky. By Stark's reckoning, a good hour and a bit more had elapsed by the time the rough ground ended at the edge of a vast and pallid swamp, where small dark men quick and wild as otters were waiting for them.

Each one took a beast by the bridle and led it, first along planks that were quickly taken up behind, leaving no trace of hoofprints, and then along some trail that was hidden in knee-deep water. There was a rank wet smell of stagnant shallows and the weedy things that love them. Low-growing trees roofed the riders with pale leaves, shutting out the starshine. Ghost-white trunks loomed faintly, crouching in the water with their knees up. It was pitch black, yet the small men waded on without pause, winding and twisting until Stark had lost all sense of direction.

They came out at last on a muddy island. Dismounting, they walked a short distance along a path with crowding shrubbery on either side, heavy with night-blooming blossoms. Stark saw a glint of light ahead, made out a long low structure all but invisible among taller trees.

Llandric, leading the way, tapped in a ritual sequence on some brittle material that was not wood.

There was a sudden burst of static inside, beyond thin walls, and a voice said clearly:

"They're spreading, getting higher. Half of Skeg must be burning."

A door opened, spilling light. A man looked out at them and said testily, "Come in, come in." He turned away unceremoniously, more interested in what was going on in the room than he was in them. As courteously as he could, to make up for it, Llandric handed the Lady Sanghalain over the threshold. Morn followed her, stooping his bare bullet head almost to his chest. Stark followed him.

The house was built of reeds, bundled and tied or woven to form the ribs and walls. The technique with which it was done was so sophisticated, the patterns so intricate, that Stark knew it must be the age-old art of the dark marsh-dwelling people. Other islands must dot the swamp, where their secret villages were hidden. If outsiders came unbidden, the inhabitants would simply retire, knowing that when the intruders became sufficiently bored with floundering and drowning, they would go away. Or if they preferred, they might smile and agree to lead a search party. The marsh-dwellers could lead it for weeks without bringing it to this particular island, with no one the wiser. No wonder the Wandsmen had not found the transceiver or Pedrallon.

The transceiver stood at the end of the long room, a simple, rugged workhorse with a practically inexhaustible power pack and foolproof controls. The metallic voice was speaking from it again, in accented Skaithian.

"The shop's been shut, Pedrallon. I may as well go home." A pause. "Hear that?"

In the background a roar of thunder split an unseen sky.

"There goes another one. I'm sixth in line."

There was a note of finality, as though he were about to sign off.

"Wait!" The man in the silk robe who sat crosslegged on the reed mat in front of the transceiver all but struck the thing in his urgency. "Wait, Penkawr-Che! Someone has come speak to you." He glanced over his shoulder, and his eyes widened as he saw Stark. "Yes. Someone has come. Will you wait?"

"Five minutes. No more. I've told you, Pedrallon—"

"Yes, yes, you have." Pedrallon had come to his feet. He was a slender man, graceful and quick, with the amber skin of the tropics. Somehow Stark was surprised that the richest, fattest, most comfortable segment of the planet's population would have produced the rebel Pedrallon, whose own people were under no imminent threat of any kind. He became aware at once of the tremendous vitality of the man, an intensity of feeling and purpose that made his dark eyes blaze with fires that were banked only by an iron will.

Pedrallon's gaze noted Sanghalain, rested briefly on Morn, fastened on Stark.

"I expected the Lady of Iubar. I did not expect you."

Llandric said, "He was there. I had to—I thought you would want—" He forced himself to make a complete sentence. "This is the Dark Man."

"I know," said Pedrallon.

Hate showed in his face, naked and startling.

157

25

In a moment the look was gone, and Pedrallon was speaking with swift urgency.

"I've been in touch with Penkawr-Che for some time. I've not been able to persuade him to join in any scheme for taking people away from Skaith. Perhaps one of you will have better luck."

Stark thrust Sanghalain forward. "Speak to him." She looked uncertainly at the black box, and he pointed to the microphone. "There."

"Penkawr-Che?"

"Make it fast."

"I am Sanghalain of Iubar in the White South. I have authority to promise you half of all my country's treasure, which is in my keeping, if you will take my people—"

The hard metallic voice cut her short. "Take them where? Where would I drop them, on what world that never heard of them and doesn't want them? They would be massacred; and if the Galactic Union caught me, I'd lose my license, my ship and twenty years of my life, along with that half of your country's treasure. The GU frowns on the smuggling of people. Besides . . ." The man took a long breath. When he spoke again, it was with the clenched-teeth distinctness of exasperation. "As I have tried repeatedly to explain, one ship could accommodate only a fraction of your population. Removing any number would require several ships and several landings, and on the second one I have no doubt that the Wandsmen would be waiting for us with a reception party. Two of your five minutes are up."

Sanghalain, flushed with anger, leaned closer to the

black box. "But surely you could come to some arrangement, if you wanted—"

"Your pardon, my lady," Stark said, and moved her firmly aside. "Penkawr-Che."

"Who is that?"

"Tell him, Pedrallon."

Pedrallon told him, each phrase as flat and cracking as a pistol shot.

"The off-worlder Stark, the Dark Man of the prophesy, come back from the north. He pulled down the Citadel. He pulled down Yurunna. He drove the Lords Protector into hiding at Ged Darod. He has been at Tregad with an army, Tregad has revolted and sent a force to Irnan to break the siege."

Penkawr-Che laughed. "So much, friend Pedrallon? Yet I hear no joy in your voice. Why is that, I wonder? Old loyalties still twining in the heartstrings?"

"I point out to you," said Pedrallon coldly, "that the situation has changed."

"It has indeed. Skeg is going up in flames, every off-worlder in the enclave has had to run for his life, and we're told that if we ever come back to Skaith, we'll be killed on sight. So?"

"So," said Stark, "I brought Simon Ashton back from the Citadel."

"Ashton?" He could picture the man in the com-room of the ship sitting bolt upright. "Ashton's alive?"

"He is. Take him to Pax, and the Galactic Union will hail you as a hero. Take as many leaders of Irnan and Tregad as you can manage, and be hailed as a humanitarian. As delegates, they can go to Pax with Ashton, and the bureaucrats will deal with all those problems you find so insoluble. They may even reward you. I can guarantee that the Irnanese will pay you well."

"And I," said Pedrallon. "I've already given you one fortune. I'm willing to give another."

"Now," said Penkawr-Che, "I'm interested. Where is Ashton?"

"On the way to Irnan."

"There'll be a battle there. I'll not risk my ship—"

159

"We'll win it."

"You can't guarantee that, Stark."

"No. But you can."

A new note in the man's voice, a poised withdrawal. "How?"

"You must have some planet-hoppers aboard."

The voice loosened somewhat. "I've got four."

"Armed?"

"Considering the places I get into, they have to be."

"That's what I thought. Do they have, or can you rig, loud-hailers?"

"Yes."

"Then all I need is four good pilots. How many passengers can you take?"

"Not above twenty this trip. My pressurized cargo space is pretty full, and cabins I have none."

"What about your colleagues? Would any of them be interested?"

"I'll ask."

The transceiver clicked and was silent.

Sanghalain had been looking at Stark. Bars of color burned on her cheekbones, and her eyes had gone all wintry, stormy gray with no sunlight. Morn loomed over her, the massive trident cradled in his hands.

"What of me, Stark? What of my people?"

He could see why she was angry with him; his action must have appeared both high-handed and ungrateful.

"Go with Ashton and the others," he said. "Plead your case at Pax. The more of you there are to ask for help, the more likely it is that the Union will grant it."

She continued to stare at him steadily. "I do not understand Pax. I do not understand the Union."

Pedrallon broke in, his voice vibrant with excitement. "There is much we cannot understand. But I propose to go, and I—"

Morn shook his head and motioned Pedrallon to silence. *My way is best for Sanghalain,* he said in Stark's mind. *Think.*

Sanghalain gave Morn a little startled glance, and then stood quietly, in an attitude of listening.

Stark thought.

He thought of Pax, the city that had swallowed up a planet: high, deep, broad, complex, teeming with its billions from all across the galaxy, frightening, beautiful, without compare.

He thought of Power, which was another name for Union. He thought of far-ranging law. He thought of freedom and peace and prosperity. He thought of ships that flashed between the suns.

As well as a man could, he thought of the Galaxy.

Infinitely swifter and more powerful than words, these thoughts passed from his mind to Sanghalain's, with Morn acting as the bridge, and he saw her expression change.

Morn said, *Enough.*

Sanghalain, wide-eyed, whispered, "Indeed, I did not understand."

"Ashton has some importance in that society. He will do all he can to help your people."

She nodded uncertainly and became immersed in her own thoughts.

The transceiver crackled. Penkawr-Che's voice came on again.

"No takers. Most of them have refugees aboard." Apparently Penkawr-Che did not. "Some have full cargoes or won't risk an open landing. You'll have to be satisfied with me. Where do we rendezvous?"

The arrangements were made.

"Keep them out from under, Stark, when I come down. They don't seem to understand things very well." Noises in the background told of another ship lifting off. "Really my turn now. Gods, you're missing something, though. A burning city is a lovely sight. I hope some of Gelmar's little Farers roast their arses in it."

A click, and silence.

Stark said, "How well do you know this man, Pedrallon? Can he be trusted?"

"No more than any off-worlder."

Pedrallon faced Stark squarely, and Stark realized that he was older than he had seemed at first glance, the smooth unlined skin masking maturity and power.

161

"No one of you has come here out of any love for Skaith. You come for your own reasons, which are selfish. And you above all have done incalculable injury to the only system of stable government my sad world possesses. You have endeavored to wrench the foundation from under an ancient building to make it topple, not for the good of Skaith, but for the good of yourself and Ashton. The good of Irnan and Tregad and Iubar is merely an accidental factor that you use for your own advantage. For this I hate you, Stark. Also, I must admit that I cannot gracefully accept the fact that men do live on other planets. I feel in my soul that we of Skaith are the only trueborn men, and all others must be less than human. But my world is ill, and like any physician I must use whatever physic is at hand to heal the patient, and so I work with you and with Penkawr-Che and his kind, who are here only to pick Skaith's bones. Be satisfied that I work with you. Do not ask for more."

He turned his back on Stark and spoke to Llandric.

"We have much to do."

Most of that "much" concerned notifying Pedrallon's network, which seemed to reach into some surprising places in spite of its thinness. Pedrallon was not disposed to give Stark any details. The Dark Man was taken to an adjoining reed house, out of earshot. Sanghalain and Morn went to another. Food was brought to Stark by one of the men, who refused to answer any of Stark's questions except to say that he was not a Wandsman. Without knowing it, he answered one question; Pedrallon was a charismatic leader who held his people as much by the force of his personality as by his clear-thinking mind. He would be valuable at Pax.

It was warm and still on the island, as Old Sun rose and made his daily journey across the sky. There was a feeling of immense peace and isolation. It was difficult for Stark to realize that he was almost at the end of his long journey, almost at the fulfillment of both his goals.

Almost.

Speculation at this point was futile. Events would bring their own solutions or lack of them. Deliberately he cleared his mind and slept, with the small sounds of the swamp in his ears, until he was called to join the others.

In the golden afternoon the dark little men led them through the watery ways, under the pale branches. They were seven when they started. Two of Pedrallon's men had already left on their separate journeys. At intervals the other two, and then Llandric, diverged and vanished among the ghostly trees, leaving troubled wakes to lap against upthrust roots. Llandric would take Sanghalain's instructions to her escort and drivers and then slip back into Ged Darod. Morn would go with Sanghalain. The bond between the sea-dwelling Ssussminh and the ruling house of Iubar was apparently both ancient and very strong.

They reached the place where they were to wait, and Pedrallon bade good-bye to his swamp-dwellers with much touching of foreheads and clasping of wrists. The little men took the beasts and melted quietly back into their private wilderness.

Morn thrust the tines of his trident into the mud, stripped off the leather garment and immersed himself in a shallow pool, lying with his eyes half covered by filmy membranes.

His voice groaned in Stark's mind like waves among hollow rocks. *I long for the cold sea.*

"At Pax you may have any environment you wish," Stark told him. A large part of the city was devoted to the comfort of nonhumans of all descriptions, some so alien that the quarters had to be sealed in with air locks and all communication done in glass-walled isolation rooms.

They settled themselves on dry ground at the edge of the pool, in a screen of rank vegetation. Beyond them was the plain, empty and peaceful in the sunlight. They were farther from Ged Darod than they had been when they entered the swamp the night before, and there was no sight of anything living.

For a long while no one spoke. Each was oppressed

with his own thoughts. Pedrallon still wore his native garment, a robe of patterned silk, but he had a red Wandsman's tunic with him in a bundle, and he carried his wand of office. Sanghalain's misty draperies were somewhat limp, her face pale and drawn. She was afraid, Stark thought, and small wonder. She was taking a tremendous step into the unknown.

"You can still change your mind," he said.

She glanced at him and shook her head. "No."

The fairy lady of the Pleasure Garden was gone. A woman was left, still beautiful, vulnerably human. Stark smiled.

"I wish you well."

"Wish us all well," said Pedrallon with unexpected vehemence.

"Doubts?" said Stark. "Surely not."

"Doubts every step of the road. I live with doubts. If this could have been done in any other way . . . I said I hated you, Stark. Can you understand me when I say that I hate myself even more?"

"I think so."

"I could not make them listen! Yet it's all there for them to see. North and south, the cold closing in, driving the outlying peoples ahead of it. The land shrinking, with ever more people to be fed from what is left. They know what must come, if they persist in forbidding any part of the population to leave."

"They stay with what they know. They can bear the slaughter. They'll still rule at the end of it, as they did after the Wandering."

"We did much good then," said Pedrallon fiercely. "We were the stabilizing force. We kept sanity alive."

Stark did not dispute him.

"My own people," Pedrallon said, "also do not understand. They think Old Sun will never desert them as he has the others. They think their temples and their sacred groves and their ivory cities will stand forever, unchanged. They think the wolves will never come down on them, sharp-toothed and starving. I am angry with them. But I love them, too."

A sound came into the quiet air.

Sanghalain looked upward, her hand over her mouth, her eyes wide.

The sunset sky roared and thundered and bloomed pale fire. The ground trembled. The limber trees were shaken by a sudden wind.

Penkawr-Che's ship came down onto the plain.

When the first of the Three Ladies rose, Stark was in a throaty-voiced planet-hopper on his way to pick up Tuchvar and the hounds.

26

There was something to be said for modern technology. Stark was glad enough to sit and watch the miles roll away far below him in the cluster light. He had toiled over a sufficient number of those miles in less comfortable ways.

The hopper was far from new, and apparently Penkawr-Che did not go in for spit and polish; nothing shone, not even the laser cannon on its forward mount. But the engines made a healthy rumble, and the rotors chewed a workmanlike path through old Skaith's relatively virgin sky. Hoppers had been banned by the Wandsmen almost from the first, partly to keep the off-worlders from spreading too wide, partly because two or three parties had been lost through unlucky landings. The Little Sisters of the Sun had caught one group on their mountain and sacrificed the lot, singing the Hymn of Life. Wild bands had eaten another group, and a third, going down to investigate some promising ruins on an island sixty miles southwest of Skeg, had been shared by the Children of the Sea. Most off-worlders were content to do their trafficking at Skeg.

The pilot was a tough-looking, stringy-muscled man

with the blue-tinted skin and elongated features of a star-race with which Stark was not familiar. He wore a gold stud shaped like an insect in his right nostril. He was a good pilot. He spoke Universal, the lingua franca, very badly and very little, which was all right. Stark was never in a chatty mood. The fellow kept glancing at him now and again, as though he thought that Stark, unshaven and still wearing the rumpled tunic he had borrowed at Tregad, was a pretty poor sort of hero.

Stark thought the blue man's skipper was a pretty poor sort of merchant captain. He had not fallen in love at first sight with Penkawr-Che, who had too much the capable look of a shark, especially when he smiled, which was too often and with his teeth only. He would not have chosen Penkawr-Che to bear shield beside him in any fight where the odds were doubtful. The man's motives were plainly mercenary, and that Stark did not hold against him as long as he kept faith. But Penkawr—the Che part only meant Captain—gave him the impression of a man whose first and only consideration would always be himself.

From these things and from his ship, the *Arkeshti*, and some of her arrangements, Stark guessed that Penkawr was one of those traders whose ventures are often indistinguishable from piracy. Still, he was Pedrallon's contact and the best there was. Like Pedrallon, Stark would have to make do.

The hopper covered the distance in a surprisingly short time. Stark saw the pilgrim roads, almost deserted this night, and the glow of Ged Darod far off in the midst of the plain. He pointed, and the pilot swung away to make a long curve over the wooded hills to the west, dropping down almost to treetop level.

There were tracks through the woods. Some led to the mountain passes, and Stark could make out straggling bands of Farers still on them, heading for Irnan. They were going to be late for the battle. Whenever the hopper went over, they rushed frantically for the imagined shelter of the trees.

166

The hopper swept out over an edge of low cliff and turned to hover, dancing like a dragonfly.

The blue man said, "Where?"

Stark studied the cliff, turning repeatedly to look off toward Ged Darod and the roads. The shining of the Three Ladies was soft and beautiful, and deceptive.

"Farther on."

The blue man nudged the craft on a quarter of a mile.

"Farther."

The pilgrims on the nearest road, tiny scattered figures, were stopping, drawn by the unfamiliar sound of thrumming motors.

Stark said, "There."

The hopper settled down.

"Take it up again," said Stark. "Keep the area clear any way you have to."

He pushed the hatch open and jumped, running through a pounding downwash as the craft rose above him.

It was a few minutes before he located the path by which he had come down the cliff. He went up along it, reckoning that the hollow where he had left Tuchvar was a couple of hundred yards off to his right. The insistent sound of the motors stayed with him, an intrusion on the silence. At the top of the cliff the dappled shadows lay thick under the trees.

Gerd's voice shouted in Stark's mind. *Danger, N'Chaka!*

Under the motor noise he heard a sound, felt movement, quick and purposeful. He gave a great leap sideways.

The screaming began almost at once. But the dagger had already flown.

Stark felt the blow and the numbing pain in his right shoulder. So much he had accomplished, that it struck there instead of at his heart or his throat. He saw the jeweled haft glinting dully, grasped it and pulled it free. Blood came welling after it, a hot wetness under his sleeve. There was a great amount of noise, bodies thrashing, sobs, cries, crashings in the undergrowth, the

167

baying of hounds. He went back onto the path, holding the dagger in his left hand.

There were two men, groveling in the extremity of terror. They wore black cloaks, and when Stark pulled the hoods back, the white unhuman faces of Fenn and Ferdic stared up at him, their night-seeing eyes stretched and agonized with fear.

Not kill! said Stark to the hounds. And aloud, "You will die if you move."

The proud white courtiers lay in the dust. They did not move except to breathe.

The hounds came crashing out into the path. Tuchvar followed, a long way behind.

"Take their weapons," Stark said. Blood dripped slowly from his fingers onto the ground. Gerd sniffed at it and growled, and the hair went up stiffly along his spine.

"The flying thing frightened the hounds," Tuchvar said, bending over the two. "Then they said you were there, and we started, and then—" He looked at Gerd, and then up at Stark, and forgot what he was doing.

"Take their weapons!"

He took them.

"Get up," Stark said.

Fenn and Ferdic rose, still trembling, staring at the thronging houndshapes in the gloom.

"Were you alone?"

"No. We had hired six assassins to help us, when we had made certain you were not among the men taken at Ged Darod. It was said that you would be found at Irnan or on the way there. We left Ged Darod, in the hope—" Fenn's breath caught raggedly in his throat. "When the flying thing went over the woods, our men fled, but we stayed to see. It is an off-world thing—yet we were told that all the ships had gone from Skaith."

"Not quite all," Stark said. He was in a fever to be rid of them. "Tell Kell à Marg that I gave you two your lives to pay for the two I was forced to take at the north gate. Tell her I will not do it another time. Now go, before I set the hounds on you."

They turned and rushed away. The dark wood swallowed them quickly.

Tuchvar said uncertainly, "Stark . . ."

Grith thrust her shoulder against the boy, forcing him back. The hounds padded restlessly, forming a fluid circle, whining in a curiously savage way. Gerd's growling rose and fell and never stopped. His eyes burned in the patches of light from the Three Ladies.

Without looking away from Gerd, Stark said to Tuchvar, "Go down to the plain."

"But I can help—"

"No one can help me. Go."

Tuchvar knew that that was true, and he went, his feet dragging.

Stark stood with his weight forward over his bent knees, his feet wide apart, the dagger in his left hand. He cared no more than a tiger which paw he used. The blood dripped steadily from his fingers. He did not dare to try and staunch it; Gerd would not give him time.

His eyes had become fully adjusted to the dim light, eyes almost as good as those of the Children. He could see the circling hounds, their jaws open, hot and eager, ready to tear him as the wounded Flay had been torn on the Plain of Worldheart. "Your flesh is vulnerable," Gelmar had said. "One day it will bleed. . . ."

It was bleeding now. The hounds had accepted him as one of themselves, not as an overlord like the Houndmaster, and he must face the inevitable consequence of his position. The pack followed the strongest, and according to law and custom, when a leader showed weakness, the next in line would try to pull him down. Stark had known from the beginning that this day would come, and he bore the hounds no ill-will because of it. It was their nature.

He could see Gerd in the pathway, huge and pale, and he thought an alien wind blew across him, bringing the chill breath of snow.

He spoke a warning. *N'Chaka still the strongest.* But that would not be true for very long.

Gerd's thoughts were incoherent. The smell of

169

blood had roused an immense and blind excitement in him. Whatever dim affection he might have conceived for Stark was drowned in that hot redness. He ripped at the ground with his claws, shifting his hindquarters back and forth with dainty movements, going through the whole ritual of challenge.

Stark, feeling weakness beginning to creep along his veins, said, *All the hounds of Yurunna not kill N'Chaka. How can Gerd?*

The bolt of fear hit Stark. The charge would follow.

Stark threw the dagger.

The blade pierced Gerd's nigh forepaw. It went on into the ground, pinning it.

The hound screamed. He tried to wrench the blade loose and screamed the more.

Stark managed to unsheathe his sword. Wild sendings of terror battered him. He forced himself to think of nothing but Gerd; Gerd's head tossing, Gerd's mouth agape, horrible with fangs. He forced himself to go forward with all the strength and quickness he could muster and touch the swordpoint to Gerd's throat, where it swelled with corded muscle above his breast.

He thrust the sharp point in, through tough hide into yielding flesh, and Gerd stiffened and looked up at him. The hound stood very still.

Stark held the blade rigid. And now Gerd's blood ran and puddled the dry dust, mingling with Stark's.

The hellhound gaze wavered, slid aside. The huge head dropped. The hindquarters sank in submission.

N'Chaka ... strongest.

Stark withdrew the sword and sheathed it. Leaning down, he plucked the dagger from Gerd's paw. Gerd cried.

A wave of giddiness went over Stark. He put his hand on Gerd's shoulder to steady himself.

Come on, old dog, he said. *We both want our hurts tended.*

He went along the path, and Gerd came on three legs beside him. The rest of the pack slunk after.

Tuchvar, who had not gone all the way, ran to meet them, busily tearing strips from his smock.

The blue man had had no trouble keeping the area clear. He had made one lazy circle toward the road and the pilgrims had fled. When he saw Stark and the boy and the pack of hounds coming down the path, he landed to take them aboard.

He did not enjoy the flight from that point on.

27

The valley of Irnan was a desolation in what should have been the fullness of approaching harvest. Besieging armies had ruined and devoured, trampled and destroyed. Not one blade of grass remained. The fields were dust, the orchards long vanished into the smoke of campfires. Only the city remained outwardly unchanged, gray and old upon its height, the walls battered by siege engines but still unbreached. Above the gate the mythic beast still reared its time-worn head, jaws open to bite the world.

Inside the walls the people of Irnan were starving. Each day voices grew more insistent, calling for surrender. Jerann and his council of elders knew that they could not hold out much longer against those voices. People died. There was no more room to bury them within the walls. There was no more wood wherewith to burn them. The bodies were thrown over the walls now for the carrion birds, and Jerann was afraid of pestilence.

On a dark still morning, between the setting of the Three Ladies and the rising of Old Sun, a wind came out of the east. It struck the encampments of the besiegers with sudden violence, scattering the bivouac fires, tearing down tents. Flames sprang up. A herd of cattle stampeded through the outlying rabble of Farers. Dust whirled in choking clouds.

Behind their stone walls the people of Irnan watched and wondered. It was a strange wind, and there was no other sign of storm under the clear stars.

For three hours the wind screamed and battered, striking now here, now there. At times it subsided entirely, as though it rested and gathered strength to strike again. When Old Sun rose, the encampments were a shambles of wrecked tents, of clothing and equipment tossed about and trampled. Men coughed and shielded their eyes from the dust. And then those in the farthest lines, looking toward the sunrise, cried out and reached for the war-horns.

A legion was there, poised and ready. They saw the leather-clad troops with their heavy spears, and the banner of Tregad leading them. They saw a company of villagers armed with bills and reaping hooks. They saw hooded men in cloaks of dusty purple, red and brown, green and white and yellow, with their lances and their many-colored pennants, and their strange long-legged beasts. They saw, off to one side, an assembly of small dark winged folk all glittering with glints of gold, their wings outstretched. All about them, standing guard, were ranks of unhuman shapes striped in green and gold and armed with tall four-handed swords.

The hollow-eyed watchers on the wall saw all this, too, though they did not at first believe it.

The small folk folded their wings, and a sound they had made, as of chanting, stopped.

The wind fell. The dust cleared. War-horns sounded, deep and snarling.

The legion charged.

The Farers, always disorganized, ran away. The mercenaries, taken as they were by surprise, were not so easily overrun. Horns and shrill-voiced pipes mustered them. Officers shouted them into line. They caught up what weapons they could find and ran through the rubbish of their encampments to meet the attackers.

Foremost among the mercenaries was a company of Izvandians, tall lint-haired warriors from the Inner Barrens with the faces of wolves. They had been quartered at Irnan at the time of the revolt, in the service of the Wandsmen, and their leader was the same Kazimni who had taken Stark and his party north.

Kazimni recognized the two who rode at the forefront of the Tregadians, beside the fierce old man who captained them, and he laughed. The man, what was his name, something short and aggressive . . . Halk. Halk was shouting the war cry that had been born that day at Irnan.

"Yarrod! Yarrod! Yarrod!"

The watchers on the city walls heard it. They too recognized the big man with the long sword. They knew the woman who rode by him armed for battle, her hair falling loose from under her cap, the color of bronze new from the forges.

"Gerrith! The wise woman has returned! Gerrith and Halk!"

Jerann, not alone, wondered about the Dark Man.

Men and women took up that war cry. Irnan became, in a matter of moments, a city of the hopeful instead of the doomed. "Yarrod! Yarrod!" they cried, and the mustering horns began to call.

The two forces joined battle.

The first charge bore the mercenaries back and scattered them. But they greatly outnumbered their attackers; and they were tough, seasoned fighting men. They rallied. A force of them drove against the left of the Tregadian line, to put a wedge between it and the tribesmen. The Fallarin, idling in reserve, shot a whirlwind against them, and in its wake the century of Tarf loosed a storm of arrows and followed that with swinging steel. The mercenaries were thrown back.

They formed again. This time they went against the Tregadians, feeling that the alien troops would desert the battle if they were beaten. The men from Tregad reeled and gave back. Old Delvor roared at them, cursing them in a voice like a trumpet. They fought furi-

173

ously, but still they were borne back by superior numbers.

Sabak rallied the tribesmen and came down at a run on the Izvandian flank. The Izvandians wheeled to meet them, forming a square bristling with lancepoints, archers in the rear ranks firing steadily. The charge of the Hooded Men faltered in a tumbling of men and mounts like a wave shattered on a sudden reef.

For the first time in months, the gates of Irnan opened and every man and woman who could still bear arms issued out to fall upon the mercenaries' rear.

To the south and east, a ragged multitude had come swarming out of the passes from the direction of Ged Darod. Old Sun knew how many thousand had left the temple city to pour across the mountains. Probably no more than half of those had finished the journey, driven by an all-consuming fever of holiness to accomplish the downfall of Irnan and the traitors who had come to her assistance. The Wandsmen who were scattered throughout the mass judged that twenty thousand would hardly tell their sum.

When Stark saw them from the air, they looked like one of the moving carpets one sees when an ant colony is on the move. Disorganized, untrained, slatternly, they were still a formidable weight of flesh to be dumped on the wrong side of the balance.

He nodded to the blue man and spoke into the microphone, to the pilots of the three hoppers flying with him.

"Let's build them a fence."

Out of the naked sky, four shapes came rushing toward the mob of Farers. Swift as dragonflies, they roared back and forth across the astounded and terrified front of the mob, striking the ground with lightnings that blinded the eye and deafened the ear, and each crack shattered rocks and trees and made the ground smoke.

A god's voice spoke from the leading shape.

"Turn back! Turn back or you will all die!"

The flying shapes began to quarter across the depth and width of the mob. God-voices spoke from all of

174

them in huge tones. "Turn back. Turn back." At the edges of the mob the ground was tortured by more lightnings.

A frenzy of cries went up. Farers knelt and lay on the ground. They milled and swirled. Even the Wandsmen did not know what to say to them in the face of this stunning power.

The flying things drew off and hung motionless in the sky, in a line across the Farer front, where the smoke and dust still rose. They waited for a time. Then they began to move slowly forward, and the licking tongues of fire cracked over the heads of the mob.

"Turn back!"

The Farers turned and streamed away in panic toward the mountains, leaving behind scores of dead, trampled underfoot.

The hoppers flew on to Irnan, where the battle swayed back and forth in dust and blood and weariness.

They flew in formation, a diamond pattern with Stark's craft at the leading point. They flew slowly and not very high because there was no weapon on the ground that could harm them. They flew over the knots and clots and ranks of struggling men, and faces turned upward to stare at them, petrified. Stark could pick out the colored cloaks of the tribesmen and the distinctive dress of some of the mercenary bands, but most of them were clad in indistinguishable leather, and in any case they were too closely engaged to pick out friend from foe.

"Anywhere you can, hit the ground," he said, "without hitting anything else. No good killing our own people."

The hoppers peeled off, each pilot pleasing himself. Laser bolts cracked and smoked around the broad perimeters of the battle, and in the open places where there were only the dead, beyond hurt. It was strange to watch how the fighting quieted and men stood still with their weapons half raised, looking upward. No one of them had ever seen a machine that flew in the air, nor any weapon that made lightning brighter than that of the sky god, and more deadly.

The four craft took up formation again, and Stark spoke into the pickup of the loud-hailer. His voice, magnified, echoing, tremendous, rang out across the field of battle.

"I am the Dark Man. I have come back from the Citadel and the prophecy of Irnan is fulfilled. You who fight against us, lay down your arms, or the lightning will strike you dead."

And he began to give orders, the hopper now darting swiftly here and there as he pointed. Orders to the captains of Irnan and Tregad and the leaders of the tribesmen to disengage and draw back.

This they did, leaving the enemy isolated.

Once more in formation, the hoppers quartered the field and voices said, "Lay down your arms or die."

On the ground Kazimni shrugged and said to his Izvandians: "We were paid to fight men, and we have done that." He sheathed his sword and tossed away his spear.

All over the field men were doing the same.

To the three pilots Stark said, "Bring them together and hold them. If any try to break out, stop them." He turned to the blue man. "Set down there by those hooded riders. Then join the others."

The hopper settled down.

Tuchvar and the hounds scrambled out. Stark followed. The blue man had given him first aid, and his wound had been cared for by *Arkeshti's* surgeon, while he waited for the three hoppers to be rigged and serviced. Penkawr-Che had given him a tunic of foreign cut that showed the color of spilled blood in the sunlight.

With Tuchvar and the hounds behind him, Stark walked toward the tribesmen, and Sabak brought him one of the tall desert beasts. He mounted.

The troop formed into line: purple Hann, brown Marag, yellow Qard, green Thorn, white Thuran, red Kref.

Fallarin and trotting Tarf fell in in their accustomed place, but this time Alderyk remained with them, leaving Stark alone with his hounds at the head of the line.

Ashton was with the Fallarin, where he had been throughout the battle; he, too, stayed.

They passed the ranks of the Tregadians, who were forming raggedly, and old Delvor shouted, "Let them go first, they've marched a long way for it!"

Halk and Gerrith left the standard of Tregad and rode beside Stark.

They rode toward the city, and the Irnanese in the field lifted weapons and cried out their names, hailing them.

Stark passed through the massive gate, beneath the dim heraldic beast. The tunnelway through the thickness of the wall was as he remembered it, dark and close. Beyond was the wide square with the gray stone buildings around it, and in the center was the platform where he had stood bound and awaiting death those months ago. Then he remembered the voice of the mob, remembered the spear that pierced Yarrod's heart, remembered Gerrith stripped of the Robe and Crown, standing naked in the sunlight. He remembered how the arrows had flighted from the windows around the square, a shining rain of death that struck down the Wandsman and signaled the beginning of the revolt.

Jerann and the elders, in threadbare gowns, their starveling faces overfilled with joy, stood waiting, and all about them crowds of tattered scarecrows wept and cheered.

So the Dark Man came back to Irnan.

28

Stark still had work to do. He left Jerann and the elders, with Gerrith and Ashton, in the council hall. He had told them about Penkawr-Che and the ship. Ashton and the wise woman could tell them all what had happened in the north. He returned to the field.

Halk rode beside him, through the filthy streets where scarecrows danced and cried and caught at them as they passed.

"I see that I must still stay my hand, Dark Man," Halk said. "If I were to kill you after this, my own people would tear me to pieces. And so I lose my revenge."

"You ought to have tried taking it before."

"The Fallarin would not have given *me* windfavor," he said bitterly. "The tribesmen would not have followed *me* after Yurunna. Because of Irnan I let you live. But I tell you this, Dark Man. I will be glad to see you gone."

And he spurred away to join the Irnanese warriors.

Pensive, Stark rode out to where the mercenary bands waited under the watchful hoppers.

He had seen the distinctive dress and the lint-white hair of the Izvandians from the air, and he was not surprised to find Kazimni leading them. He had come to like that man on the cold journey across the Barrens. And he bore him no grudge for having sold the little party from Irnan into captivity with the trader Amnir, in the hope of sharing a great profit when they were delivered to the Lords Protector. Kazimni had not taken any oath of loyalty to them, and Stark had known perfectly well what he was doing. Force of circumstance, not Kazimni, had entrapped them.

"You had poor return on your trading venture," he said, "and here you are again, leaving Irnan empty-handed. The place seems unlucky for you."

Kazimni smiled. He had slanting yellow-gray eyes and pointed cheekbones, and he wore the torque and armband of a chieftain.

"Perhaps the third time will be better, Dark Man."

"There will be a third time?"

"As certainly as there will be winter. The Wandsmen are not so easily beaten. They'll gather new forces, stronger and better organized. They have learned now that their precious Farers are of little use. There will be war, Stark."

"If things go well out there among the stars, power will pass from the hands of the Wandsmen."

"There will still be war."

"Perhaps." Stark thought that Kazimni was right. But he said, "For the present, go in peace."

They struck hands, and the Izvandians marched away. One by one the other bands of mercenaries followed. The hoppers escorted them out of the valley.

Stark rode the battlefield.

The Irnanese troops and the men of Tregad were working together, carrying supplies into the starving city from the abandoned stores, gathering the dead and wounded, rounding up livestock. The tribesmen had come out to look after their fallen and to loot the ravaged encampments. Stark did not begrudge them what they found. There were enough dusty cloaks strewn about the field, a long way from home.

When he was satisfied, Stark returned to the city in search of Ashton.

He found him in one of the chambers in the great stone pile that contained the council hall. Ashton, thin and windburned but still fit, looked at him a moment and then said:

"You've decided to stay, haven't you?"

"Until the ships come. Kazimni believes there will be war again as soon as the Wandsmen can gather up new forces. I think he's right, and I don't like leaving a job half done."

"Well," said Ashton, "I won't argue with you, Eric; and I suppose you might as well be risking your neck here for a while longer as on some other godforsaken planet."

Then he added, "I don't suppose you knew it, but Jerann asked Gerrith to go with the delegation to Pax, and she refused."

"I didn't know it," Stark said, "but I won't pretend I'm not glad to hear it."

He went to the hall to speak with Jerann and the elders. There was great activity, people coming and

179

going, tending to the needs of the city. Jerann, in the midst of it, seemed to have shed ten years since Stark saw him in the square.

"I am grateful," the old man said, when Stark had told him his decision. "We shall all feel safer with you here at Irnan."

"Very well, then," Stark said. "I can handle one of the flying things. When you bargain with Penkawr-Che for the price of your passage, bargain for that also. Then Irnan will have a powerful weapon, and far-seeing eyes, and a radio to speak with the ships when they come."

The council agreed. Only Halk was not pleased, looking at Stark in a certain way, so that limping Gerd began to growl.

Stark's thoughts were elsewhere. "Where is the wise woman?"

No one knew.

The tribesmen and the Fallarin, not wishing to be housed in the noisome city, had made their separate encampments away from it. Stark visited them.

The tribesmen were well satisfied. They had considerable loot left by the mercenaries, and the elders had promised them much besides. They were content to remain with Stark.

The Fallarin would not commit themselves. Only Alderyk said:

"I will stay with you, Dark Man. Two of my people will go to this world you call Pax to see and observe and bring back news to me. We shall make our decisions when it pleases us. For the moment, at least we are secure in the north. As for Irnan, we shall see. I promise nothing, and my folk are free to return to the Place of Winds at any time they wish."

"But you yourself will stay."

Alderyk smiled his edged and mocking smile.

"I told you, Stark. Mine to control the whirlwind."

Three of the hoppers flew off to Tregad with Delvor and his aides. They would carry the news of the victory and fetch back with them such of the leaders of Tregad as wished to make the trip to Pax. The fourth hopper was maintaining radio contact with Penkawr-Che's *Arkeshti*, orbiting just outside the atmosphere. Not he to risk his ship until the area chosen for landing was completely cleared.

It was night when *Arkeshti* came in, dropping down through the glow of the Three Ladies, and all of Irnan was on the walls to watch.

Penkawr-Che, a long lean Antarean with skin like burnished gold and a crest of stiff-curling hair, came to the hall with Pedrallon and did his talking with Ashton and the elders. He made no difficulty about the hopper, and the spare power pack Stark requested.

Stark still did not like him.

Next day Stark went aboard the ship with Ashton to inspect the quarters the crew had been busy jury-rigging in an empty hold.

"This will do," said Ashton. "Anything will do that gets me away from Skaith." He took Stark's hand. They had already held their post mortems on all that had happened and said their farewells in the privacy of Ashton's room, sitting very late over a jug of captured wine. Now all Ashton said was, "We'll be as fast as we can. Have you seen Gerrith?"

"No. But I think I know where she is."

"Go find her, Eric."

The others were coming aboard. Stark spoke briefly to Sanghalain and Morn, and Pedrallon, and left the ship. He sent Ashton's mount back to the city with Tuchvar and Sabak, who had ridden out with them to stare wide-eyed at the ship. Then he rode away up the valley.

He had come this way only once before, at the start of the long journey, but it was not difficult to follow the road or to note the place where he must leave it to find the grotto. The wanton armies had ravaged even here, stripping the land for forage and firewood. He left his mount below the grotto and climbed the steep path.

Inside it was dark and cool, with the tomb-smell of places that never see the sun. The grotto had served generations of Gerriths, wise women of Irnan. When Stark had seen it before, there had been rugs and hangings, lamps, braziers, furniture, the great bowl that held the Water of Vision. Now the place was empty, naked, gutted.

He called her name. It echoed in the vaulted rooms.

She came from an inner chamber where one candle burned.

"Why did you run away?"

"I did not wish to see you go. And I did not wish in any way to persuade you not to go."

She waited, and he told her his decision.

"Then you see, I was right to come here." She came close and touched him. "I'm glad."

"So am I. But why did you decide not to go to Pax, when Jerann asked you?"

"I don't really know. Except that when I saw myself walking toward the ship, a barrier came between and I could not pass it. My trip will be made another time. There is something more I must do here, first."

She smiled, but he could not see her eyes in the shadowed cave.

"What is this thing you must do?"

"I don't know that, either. And I'm not going to think about it now."

He took her into his arms, and then in a little while they went out into the light of Old Sun and heard the thunder and watched the distant flame as *Arkeshti* lifted off, outward bound for Pax.

"We must send word north," Stark said, "to Hargoth and the People of the Towers, to tell them that the star-roads will soon be open."

182

About the Author

Leigh Brackett has been writing outstanding science fiction since 1940 when her "Martian Quest" was published in *Astounding*. She is best known for her heroic adventures, featuring larger-than-life swashbucklers like Eric John Stark—her most famous character and hero of *The Ginger Star*. In addition to sf, Leigh Brackett has a long list of screenplay credits at major Hollywood studios. Her first screen assignment was a collaboration with William Faulkner of the screen adaptation for *The Big Sleep*. Ironically, her most recent screenplay was *The Long Goodbye*, a remake of that earlier classic. *The Long Goodbye* has been selected by several top critics as one of the best films of the year.

Born in Los Angeles, Leigh Brackett and husband Edmond Hamilton, a top sf writer in his own right, divide their time between the family farm in Ohio and a home in California. She is now at work on the third book of Stark's adventures. In addition Leigh Brackett will be editing for Ballantine *The Best of Planet Stories*, anthologies of stories from that memorable magazine in which Eric John Stark first appeared.